Eggemoggin
Reach Review

Volume I

An Anthology of Prose and Poetry by members of
The Deer Isle Writers' Group
&
The Eggemoggin Writers' Collaborative

EDITORS

PUBLISHED BY
Eggemoggin Reach Review
PO Box 376, Deer Isle, Maine 04627

PRINTED IN USA

Eggemoggin Reach Review ISBN 0-9755586-0-9

Eggemoggin Reach Review is available by mail for $17.95, including postage. Use the order form in the back of the book, or send $17.95 via US mail: Eggemoggin Reach Review, 32 Burnt Cove Road, Stonington, ME 04681.

CONTENTS

Contents

CONTENTS

Acknowledgments

There were three people who originated the idea for this book: Sandy Cohen, Hendrik Gideonse, and Janet King. They were joined by a Steering Committee consisting of Diane Berlew, Anne Burton, Sucha Cardoza, Jean Davison, Maureen Farr, Brenda Gilchrist, Gayle Hadley, Nancy Hodermarsky, Deborah Marshall, Norma Sheard, and Jan Thomson.

Then there are the 28 writers who submitted their best work, in poetry, fiction, and non-fiction.

And, there is a huge circle of friends and family who have supported and encouraged all of us throughout our lives.

Eggemoggin Reach connects Penobscot Bay and Jericho Bay, and flows between Deer Isle and the mainland. We chose the name *Eggemoggin Reach Review* because our contributing authors live, and write, on both sides of this beautiful body of water.

Eggemoggin Reach Review

Volume I

Sunset Over Eggemoggin Reach

Wednesday. Driving home from dinner
your husband recites all he is learning
about stonework for the foundation
he plans to build, and all he thinks
about every stone wall you pass
at your favorite seafood restaurant,
along this road where stones
seem almost to walk themselves
to the edge of the property.

You are caught in the bedrock of thought
induced by a flickering glimpse
of late sun, Camden Hills, water
blipping through early spring trees
still shivering, while his voice
barely pauses for breath and becomes one
with the hum of the motor.

What you think is the sun burning low,
ahead and to the left, becomes a dragon
flaming the barrens, mid-April, low wind,
the fire leaves its trail of ash
and the asphalt pulls you into
the sinking sun, so when the fading light
parts the trees, you cannot help
but pull over. He begins his dissertation
on fire, on spring burning:
the safeties, the hazards.

You are watching the deep dusk sky
fall into an iodine sunset, and are willing
to weep for the color alone and the shadow
of the hills, and the water, like mercury,
cool and still, finding a white light
the sky doesn't offer. He urges you
to the next hill with the promise

of a better view, but you are grateful
to receive this gift-wrapped day
at this moment in this spot, relishing
the light, the color, the flames,
the scorch, his voice, the car humming,
humming, humming...

—Judi K. Beach

Night Rides

When August sweltered and the air hung thick
as wet cotton and no breeze dared disturb
the maples in their heavy green comfort,
when hollyhocks and cosmos drooped under
unrelenting sun, those days when men refused
to mow lawns and women wouldn't bake bread,
when children swagged from tired swings and
water in the wading pool was warmer than bath,

we packed into the two-toned Dodge, my sister and I
hogging the half-opened windows of the back seat;
my mother cocked the cozy wing so the speed
would breeze across her face; my father's left arm crooked
out his window, a practice never allowed his daughters,
and we rode up Alexandria Pike past the familiar
stores and homes and into the sweep of farmland.

Those hot evenings I held my face to the wind
while the sun dragged the light westward
pulling a shade on the day. Kneeling on the seat,
I stared out the back window and watched
where we had just been disappear into starred night.
Most times I followed the rising light of moon
window to window until, having cooled
with the onset of evening, I curled in the seat to sleep.

The car stopped. The engine quit. Night air
swooped in the opening doors. A small exchange
of talk between my parents. The seat flopped forward
as my father bent into the car, lifted me, carried me
in the house to my bed where I slumped on the edge,
and he removed my shoes and socks, my shirt and shorts
and left me to sleep in my underwear. I used to love
those hot night rides when we were a family
riding for relief into the coming darkness.

—*Judi K. Beach*

The Magic Insomnia of Dreams

As the body gives up its pains and tucks itself into sleep,
and the eyes close out the heavy-lidded moon, and the mind
releases its logic like a bird caged too long, and the heart
comforts them all behind a dark canopy, the consciousness
is left with nothing to do but wander its own planet that seems
almost like a painting by Chagall, one with a bright red cow
looking you right in the eye, or like something seen
on a train ride through de Chirico. Sleep consciousness
does not require elements of design and balance, for it
can fold around the edge of a cubist nude and find itself
looking at your desk in your old place of work, then
walking down a hall crowded with refrigerators to a bathroom
with small stalls, no doors and seats as high as bar stools.
The consciousness falls into step behind a child dancing
the May pole and doesn't question why it cannot find the key
to the cage a mother wears over her head, or the way
it might be walking stone to stone over a steep brook and step
onto the back of an armadillo that bucks like an unbroken steed,
the consciousness stumbling onto stairs that take flight. All night
reality constructs itself from blocks the mind has left strewn
on the floor until the sun breaks the eastern window,
and the heart throws open its bedding, and the stiff body
rises to its shower, a cup of coffee, and the mind kicks in
to read the headlines or the comics, and the consciousness
constrains itself again to a single set of tracks that stretch straight
    to the western horizon.

—Judi K. Beach

The Man Who Thought He Could Live Alone

after the painting by Rob Shetterly

At first they sat together, or lay, wrapped
in their relationship like an afghan awash
with their personalities. He was so comfortable
in her arms he forgot she wasn't a couch,
and she let him relax in her soft hold.

As he grew more accustomed, he began
to not-notice her until inertia kept him
in her easy embrace long after the tube
of television had burned out. Long after
their passion, too, spent. She became
his own personal piece of furniture, the place
where he could lie in comfort, pick up a book
and imagine he were somewhere else.

And she believed him, quietly reclining
under him, maintaining her conservative façade.
Before long she swallowed her tongue and forgot
how to speak. And he forgot to ask her
how her day was. Then he forgot she was there
and took the old green chair she used to sit on
and nailed it to the wall, forgetting its purpose,
seeing it now as a confluence of careful lines.

And so it went, she, unspeaking,
but becoming restless beneath him; he
becoming restless with the occasional thunk
and thud in his couch, experiencing it much
as a woman expects a fetus to kick, adjusting
to a space too small to nurture a self.

The thud and thunk grew into a rocking,
and then began the sudden thrusts that shoved him
to discomfort. Until one night he deja-vued a voice
muffled somewhere behind him (beneath him?)

14

and he put down his anonymous book and rose
from the couch feeling like another man,
older now, which he accepted.

As he walked away, a slow ripping began.
At first there was just the glint of steel, but then
the shaft. The hilt, her hand. She was giving birth
to her whole self through the upholstery
of the couch he had just abandoned, the couch
she would never fit into again.

—*Judi K. Beach*

Hansie Discovers the Underearth and Mr. Snitzel

Diane Berlew

Hansie lived on an island. The ocean was in front of his house, and the woods were behind it. His mother always told him not to go swimming alone or so far into the woods that he couldn't see the house. In the woods there was a fir tree in a small clearing. He could still see the house from where the tree stood, but it seemed far away. He liked to take a peanut butter sandwich and some juice and sit in the clearing next to the tree to eat.

One morning as he left the house with his lunch in a bag, his mother told him to be careful, as she usually did. Hansie said he would be. He tried to be careful, but sometimes he wished he could do something really exciting or different or special. Being careful all the time seemed a little boring.

On this visit to his tree, he crawled under the lowest branches to see what the clearing looked like from under there. It was scratchy and not very comfortable. He started to wriggle out when he felt the ground move slightly and then a little more. Suddenly he was falling slowly through dark space. He didn't feel scared, just a little dizzy. He landed with a thump on a pillow. Standing next to him was a strange looking man not much bigger than he was. He had a long nose and a big smile. His clothes were green. He was barefoot and was holding a lit candle.

"Hello, my name is Mr. Snitzel."

"I'm Hansie. Where am I?"

"This is the Underearth of the woods. Very few people have been here. I never go up to your Upperearth, but I have seen your tree once. I got a little nervous when I stuck my head up to take a look. It was all so huge and bright and windy up there. I am glad you found your way down here. I guess you're a very adventuresome boy to have found the secret entrance."

"I found it kind of by accident, but I'm really glad I did."

Mr. Snitzel guided Hansie toward a small, almost round, blue door.

"Come on into my workshop. I was just about to get the ceiling painted. I think it should be blue like the door, but first we need more light."

He opened a box of matches that Hansie hadn't noticed; in fact, he was sure it hadn't been there and had just dropped into Mr. Snitzel's hand. The matches jumped out of the box, scratched their heads on the side and flew up all alight to the ceiling and lit sixty-two candles that hung there.

"Wow. I need to learn how to do that."

"Our Underearth equipment just won't work in the Upperearth. The matches disappear. It is strictly for use down here."

Hansie decided not to tell anyone about the Underearth, except maybe his mom if she promised not to tell anyone else. If he did take magic matches home and show them to people, it would be pretty hard to explain.

They were in a room filled with all kinds of very interesting things. There were shelves covering all the walls, full of books and boxes with fancy labels that had some words Hansie could read like 'bite,' 'flying,' 'amazing,' 'open with caution,' 'share,' 'leave this alone,' and 'lucky you.'

There were bits and pieces of machines that Hansie had never seen before. He touched one gently and it sputtered, "Owowowowowowowowowo!"

"Oh be quiet. You're not hurt," said Mr. Snitzel.

The machine stopped and Hansie looked around some more at piles of fruit and vegetables and baskets of nuts and seeds. Hansie reached his hand into the basket of pumpkin seeds. He jumped back when some of the seeds whirled and spun around then dropped back in the basket lined up to spell out, "We're sleeping."

Hansie had dozens of questions to ask, but everything was so unusual that he decided to wait awhile and see what else happened.

Mr. Snitzel took a piece of the machinery with a very long screw at one end. He carried it up a narrow ladder that wasn't leaning against anything but didn't wobble. He drilled a hole quite quickly in the ceiling. Hansie was surprised to be able to see the blue sky through the hole, but he was getting very used to being surprised

"Lovely day up there," Mr. Snitzel said as he climbed down, went to one of the baskets, and picked up a walnut. He lifted the top half of the walnut off and held the bottom half so Hansie could see. There was a bug asleep under a tiny blanket.

"This is Charles. He helps me when he can stay awake."

The bug yawned and opened his big bug eyes. He looked at Hansie and winked at him. Hansie grinned and said, "Hi." He had tried to talk to bugs before, but they had never paid any attention.

Mr. Snitzel carefully lifted Charles out of his bed and sat him on the palm of his hand. Charles stretched and all of his little feet started to grow bigger and bigger and bigger. His wings unfolded, and he stood up on his huge feet.

"Would you like to start painting the ceiling sky blue?" Mr. Snitzel asked.

"Sure would," answered Charles.

Mr. Snitzel gave him a little toss into the air. Charles flew out of the hole in the ceiling, stamped his big feet in the sky, then zoomed back in and stamped on the ceiling. Each time he went in or out of the hole he flew faster and stamped harder. Soon he was just a buzzing blue blur. The ceiling was quickly turning a beautiful sky blue that looked more like sparkling dust than wet paint.

When it was finished, Charles slowed down and landed on Mr. Snitzel's outstretched hand, which was full of chocolate chip cookie crumbs. In the other hand, there was an acorn cap full of milk. While Charles ate the crumbs and drank the milk, his feet slowly shrank. Mr. Snitzel tucked the bug back into his walnut bed and carefully put the top half of the walnut back on and brushed the blue dust from his hands. Charles sighed, said goodnight in a big deep voice, and fell asleep. Hansie looked up at the ceiling again and noticed that the hole was no longer there.

"How do you think it looks?"

"W-a-a-y cool, but I think I better go home now or my mom will worry. I had a great time. May I come again?"

"Come whenever you can."

Mr. Snitzel opened the door for Hansie and flipped a pillow out after him. Hansie guessed he should sit on it, and was gently lifted into the darkness. After a little scratchiness on his head, he was back under his tree. As he walked home through the woods, he decided that being careful wasn't as boring as he had thought.

Return

The Augusta traffic circles spin me onto Route 3
The mountains rise to the East
The blue lakes define the miles to the west
My eyes search for the first glimpse of Penobscot Bay.
My throat tightens, my breath catches,
My heart slows, then quickens,
   Belfast, Searsport, Bucksport.

The narrow roads wind through
   Orland, Penobscot, Sedgwick.
I climb Caterpillar Hill
The steep arch of the Deer Isle Bridge.
The causeway curls me on to my island, dear island.
I hasten around the coves,
   Smalls, Goose, Crockett.

The final bend in the road
A giant granite boulder
Farmhouse
Lighted porch
Wood stove
Purring tomcat
   In my lap.

—Anne Larkosh Burton

Solitary Dove

A dove sits on a wire
Outside my back door
Morning and evening she is there
She makes no sound
Just sits.

She is gone now
Off hunting food, a mate,
Her children, companionship, hope,
Anything to end the loneliness
I wish I could fly.

—*Anne Larkosh Burton*

Falling In Love

Anne Larkosh Burton

I did not plan to fall in love that summer. Approaching the three score and ten point in my life, I'd lived through a divorce, the death of a spouse and a variety of other relationships. Passion required too much energy and too many risks. It was something best experienced in memory.

My life seemed settled now. I owned a comfortable home in a New York suburb and was established and respected in my profession as a psychotherapist. I enjoyed close relationships with my adult daughters and had many friends with whom I went to the theater, concerts and museums.

Perhaps it was the abundance of people in my life that made me decide to get away by myself for awhile. A cottage I once rented with my daughters in a small fishing village on an island off the coast of Maine seemed a good place to retreat and spend time reflecting on my life and sorting through my priorities. Perhaps I would even do some of the writing I was always talking about but never seemed to fit into my schedule. It was not exactly the ideal hunting ground for a new love, but then, I was not looking. Or so I thought.

Late one July, I loaded my car with the essentials: laptop, journals, books, portable radio/CD player and a stack of CDs; and enough food, toilet paper, and comfortable clothes to last me a week. Driving my old, red BMW up the Garden State Parkway, a thought surprised me: *What if I never come back?* The psychotherapist part of me filed that away for some future time. For now I was on vacation.

I slipped a new Eva Cassidy CD into the player. As I approached the toll-gate on the Tappan Zee Bridge, Eva sang a refrain that cut through me,

"I never thought I'd get this old,
Never had a reason to live so long
And the Lord's been like my shadow
Even when I was wrong,
No, I never thought it would turn out this way."

(Excerpt from "Anniversary Song," by Steven M. Digman)

What could a singer who had died before she reached the age of 35 possibly know about growing old? But the lyrics rang true; I'd made my share of mistakes and missteps, but always felt the shadow of protection around me.

* * *

The dirt lane to the small cottage wound through tall pines. I could hear the sound of the waves as they broke over the boulders on which the house was perched, some twenty feet above mean-high tide. The mandatory stack of seasoned firewood stood by the back door. The large stone fireplace invited me to take the chill off the furniture by lighting the fire that had been laid there. Two picture windows on the front of the house framed the scene of Mark Island Lighthouse and the Camden Hills across the bay.

Slipping on a sweater, I stepped out on the small cement deck. The air was fresh and smelled of salt. I pulled the sweater around me as the sun began to set and the air chilled. I wanted to sit forever in the worn Adirondack chair and listen to the sound of the water against the rocks below.

The sun comes up early Downeast, but it was the puttering engines of the lobster boats that woke me at four the next morning. I made a cup of coffee and took it out on the deck to watch the lobstermen move from buoy to buoy. As they came in close to the rocks below, I could see the captain skillfully catch the line attached to the lobster trap and feed it though the winch which hauled the trap over the low gunnel. With no wasted motion he emptied it of its contents, measured the lobsters, tossed the old bait out for the seagulls and reset the trap. The boats pulled away, heading for the next marker, and the traps slid back into the water. Sometimes the crew waved and I returned the greeting.

And I fell in love.

For several days, I wrapped myself in the simplicity of watching the water and sea birds, reading, writing and listening to music. The thought that had sprung into my consciousness as I first headed north returned. What IF I never went back! Deep inside I longed to live surrounded by this peace and beauty.

Later in the week I walked to town and began to ask people working in the shops if they lived here year round and what it was like. There were knowing smiles with the replies of "it's better in the winter," "quieter," "more peaceful," and "you can be as busy as you want to be." I inquired and learned that there were houses available that I could afford to buy.

When I returned to New Jersey, I told my family and friends of my decision to move to Maine. Some were shocked and disbelieving. They suggested, "everybody thinks they want to live where they vacation, it's just a phase."

Others were supportive and encouraging. Among them were my daughters. Although they were sad at the thought of the miles this would put between us, they wanted me to be where I would be happiest.

The hardest part was telling patients and helping them to adjust to what that would mean for their treatment. Some decided to transfer to another therapist, others were close enough to completion so our work turned to saying goodbye. There were a few who wished to continue with me on an abbreviated schedule or by phone. I was not yet ready to shed my identity as a therapist, so this provided me with some continuity.

Within a year, I sold my New Jersey house and packed my belongings and said farewell to friends and patients. With the help of my daughters, I moved into an old farmhouse on a cove in Penobscot Bay.

Three years later I still watch the tides change, the lobster boats come and go and the sun set over the Camden Hills. My view is my companion. It is always the same but ever changing. And I have a passion in my heart that feeds my soul. Occasionally I play the Eva Cassidy CD and think, "No, I never thought it would turn out this way."

Puzzles and Ashes

Sucha Cardoza

When I went out with my dogs this morning, there was a hint of smoke in the air that seemed alien to the season. Otherwise, it was clear. I could see across to the mainland. "Noreen must have fired her wood stove early," I said to myself. "Roland's doing poorly, and she's built a fire to warm him." I pictured him sitting in the easy chair next to the stove, his feet up on the fender. Noreen sometimes puts him there, to make a change from the daybed. He can see out the window better and watch for the occasional passerby on Passamaquoddy Road. And she can keep on eye on him, while she sits at the folding table to work on her jigsaw puzzles.

She has almost finished the latest: Under an indigo sky, a gentleman in frock coat and top hat helps a lady in picture hat and hoop skirts descend from a horse-drawn carriage in front of a church that lacks only a steeple to complete the picture. Noreen will probably have it finished by tomorrow. She's good at puzzles. She does lots of them.

Beneath the folding table is the portable sewing machine upon which, come winter, Noreen will stitch together the scraps of fabric people save for her. The rest of the year, it is kept in the carrying case that she has never carried anywhere. Indeed, until recently, she'd hardly ever been off-island, except to Elksport on the church bus for the annual revival in July. And once to the VA Hospital in Togus, when Roland first took sick.

Lately, though, she's become quite a traveler. When the visiting nurse takes Roland to the clinic on the mainland so his blood can be replenished, Noreen goes along, too. Three pints of blood a month keep Roland going. "Where does it go?" he asks. He holds up his hands to show they are without blemish. You can almost see through them, against the light, but nothing can leak out. His wounds are not visible. The cause of his suffering is hidden. Roland is bewildered. Behind the thick glasses, his eyes look scared, I think. But I can't be sure. Perhaps the magnifying lenses make the pupils only seem to overwhelm the irises.

Three pints of blood keep Roland going, from bed to chair and back again. On good days, he puts his coat on over his pajamas and crosses the road to the mailbox – an act of defiance and courage, for the summer people drive on Passamaquoddy Road as if it were their private access to the Colony down on the Point. And Roland is not fleet. He has grit, but no dash. He must lie down after each excursion.

Noreen's another story: Except when she's working on her puzzles or at her sewing machine, she's always bustling about. She seems unable to lie down or sit still. Although, come to think of it, she'd lie right down on the floor of the church bus, when it crossed over the bridge to the mainland, so she could not look out and see the water far below. Nevermind that the siding's so high, you could not see over if you wanted to. No telling her that. No, she'd lie on the floor of the bus, begging God to hold the bridge up till she got across. And, do you know, He heard her? Noreen's God is merciful.

I don't think she lies down on the floor of the visiting nurse's van, though. She's probably used to the trip by now, she's done it so many times. Or maybe she just doesn't care anymore. Roland, on the other hand, has taken up lying down in earnest. When he's not sitting in the easy chair, he lies on the daybed, propped on pillows, listening for the cars that speed up and down the road in the summer; for the lumbering snowplow in winter. Once I took a friend to visit him, and afterward she asked, "What does he do all day?" I thought it an obtuse question. I did not know what to say. "He thinks," I think I said. But I do not really know what fills his mind. Perhaps nothing. Perhaps it is emptying itself, like his body.

By the time I whistled up the dogs and turned back, an umber fog had settled on the Island. The smell of char was heavy in it. It was difficult to breathe. I was anxious to get home. I put the dogs on their leads and hurried them across the fields to the house. Indoors, I turned on the radio and listened to the news. A huge forest was burning, far to the north, in Canada. Smoke from the fire had spread over most of the state, but easterly winds were expected to drive it off the coastal regions by evening. And, sure enough, at twilight I could see the mainland again. The weather had turned. But the winds that carried the smoke out to sea had carried off summer, too. It was cold. I brought in what was left of last year's woodpile, enough logs for the night. I don't need more, for I am leaving the Island tomorrow. I do not know when I will return.

Tonight, I will sit up late listening to the winds rise and fall, roiling and keening as they must when the tall meadow grasses are bent under drifts that would come to your waist, were you here. Higher, even: to your chest and your shoulders, should you turn off Passamaquoddy Road and dare down the trackless lane on a gray day just after dusk, walking deeper and deeper, the wind at your back, toward the house where drawn curtains billow, a door swings on its hinges, and sleet hisses through the shutters, "I am here, open up, let me in."

Silent confession

Sandy Cohen

A t 2:00 AM on the coldest morning of January, I was taken by jet heli-
copter to the emergency room of Eastern Maine Medical Center, in
Bangor. I was treated for a heart attack. That meant immediate car-
diac surgery and the placement of two stents in a coronary artery. A year later,
I had a defibrillator implanted in my chest to monitor my heart rate and, if ever
I need it, to deliver a life-saving "therapy" of 14,000 volts.

"What does it feel like when a therapy happens?" I asked.

The cardiac surgeon who did the implant said, "It's like being hit in the
chest by a brick. The therapy makes some people fall. Others just pass out.
You'll certainly know it when it comes."

My defibrillator never went off and after 14 months of inactivity, I forgot
all about it.

Recently, I was in a different hospital, a smaller one closer to my island
home, for a test that would have been routine except for the defibrillator. The
test procedure, which started at 6:30 AM, was performed by Dr. Ross, a surgeon, assisted by a complete surgical staff in an operating theatre. This was
more involved than I had expected, since this test is fairly simple and usually
performed as an outpatient procedure. Dr. Ross, whom I had met previously,
was fully gowned and scrubbed. He introduced me to two anesthesiologists,
also gowned and scrubbed. The first, Dr. Pauling, was there to turn off my
defibrillator for the duration of the procedure. He did this by holding his stethoscope over the device while placing a specialized magnet on my chest. He
explained, "The defibrillator emits a soft beep when it turns off. I can hear it
with this," indicating the frigid bell of the stethoscope.

"I'm going to inject Demerol now. You will relax and feel nothing. If you
want to sleep, that's fine," Dr. Ritansky, the other anesthesiologist, told me.

The medical team was talking, I could hear them, but almost immediately
I realized that while I was not actually sleeping, I felt nothing. I must have
fallen asleep, because when the procedure was over, I was feeling very groggy.

Dr. Pauling returned with the stethoscope and the magnet. His mask was off and I could see that he was a young man. He looked at me. "Are you OK?"

I smiled weakly.

"I can't hear the beep," Dr. Pauling said after several minutes of holding the stethoscope in various places on my chest. "It's supposed to beep when it's back on, and it didn't beep."

"Is it the same beep as the OFF?" Dr. Ritansky asked.

"On this model, it's supposed to be a faster beep rate for ON. Now I can't tell if it's on or off. I can't release him unless I know for sure that it is on and working properly." Dr. Pauling's voice was agitated and louder. "I better get somebody from Guidant to plug him in to one of their computers and make certain it's turned on. I'll call the factory; see who they've got in Maine."

"Meantime, I'll arrange to put him into a recovery room until they get here," Dr. Ross said.

I was put on a gurney and wheeled to the recovery room. It was very cold. I wanted a blanket.

Dr. Ross came by a short time later. "Luckily, there's a Guidant engineer in Bangor attending surgical defibrillator implantations for two patients. But, they probably won't get here until the late afternoon. Therefore, I'm going to admit you to the hospital for the day. Is that OK for you?"

"That's fine with me. I'm exhausted. I hardly slept last night, and I'm still woozy from the remains of the Demerol. I'd love to be able to sleep for awhile. Could I get a blanket, please?"

I was wheeled to the elevator and taken to another wing of the hospital. Two orderlies lifted me to a bed in a two-person room.

The other patient, a slight man in his late seventies, with white hair and thin pale face was already in the room sitting in a chair between the beds. He was dressed in a blue paisley robe. He silently watched me being lifted into my bed. A nurse appeared with an intravenous drip for me. "This will keep you hydrated, it's only saline solution," she said. The nurse then covered me with a hot blanket, which felt great after the refrigeration of the recovery room. I luxuriated in the hospital bed, stretching and enjoying the comfort of the hot blanket. The nurse returned with some apple juice and another blanket.

I sat up and turned to see my new roommate, who moved his hand a little in a friendly wave of welcome.

"My name is Alexander," I said.

He extended his hand, which I shook, thinking it cold, dry and bony. His grip was faint and without power. He said nothing.

"What's your name, please?" This seemed to embarrass him, because he looked down and slouched deeper into the chair. He grunted and made a forced humming sound that went up and down as though he were trying to pronounce his name.

I realized then that verbal communication was impossible. I lay back into my pillows. "I'm glad to meet you."

Just then a heavy, grey-haired woman in her late fifties wearing blue jeans and a shiny purple jacket with gold stitchery on the back indicating that she had once visited "Dollywood," entered the room. She was accompanied by a teen-age girl, wearing an earring through her lower lip. They walked quickly past me to the man in the chair.

"Let's get you back in that bed, Wendell. You shouldn't be out." I could see the woman gripping the old man's arm to get him up from the chair and moved to his bed. "Lois, you fluff Grampa's pillows."

As they settled the man in his bed, they moved a rolling bed table toward me. On it I could see two books. One, on its side, was a black hardcover Bible with wine-red page-ends and a red ribbon page marker sticking out. The other, also a hardcover book, stood slightly open and upright. It had a color-tinted picture of Jesus, in a radiant gold halo, resembling the kind of icon that might be seen at the Hermitage. Also on the table was a yellow pad of paper and a ball point pen.

The man pointed to the beaker of water on the sink. The young woman poured him a glass and arranged the straw so he could sip the water. The older woman sat in the chair and started to leaf through a *People* magazine that she had pulled from her shoulder bag.

"Did they call the church, Wendell? Oh, Christ, you wouldn't know." The older woman seemed annoyed. "Lois, go down to the nurses' station and find out if the priest is coming."

Lois returned with a nurse.

"Well, when is the priest coming?"

"Father Gallagher is out of town just now. Another priest is going to come by this afternoon, when he gets a chance. The church called about an hour ago. There is a chapel on the ground floor, if you want to have Mr. Reese meet the priest there. We can get transportation to take him."

"What do you mean, 'When he gets a chance'?" the woman interrupted the nurse. "He's supposed to hear his confession, for Christ's sake. Oh, great, the chapel. He can't even get to the bathroom and you're gonna take him all the way down to the chapel. Yeah, right!"

The nurse shrugged her shoulders and left.

The younger woman went with her. "I'm gonna go to the gift shop, Mom."

It was quiet at last. I was able to pull up my covers and, with the warmth of the hot blanket, slept the rest of the morning.

When an attendant brought in a tray of food for lunch, I awoke. The smell of chicken noodle soup and a hamburger brought my appetite into immediate focus. I glanced at my roommate and discovered that a nurse was helping him eat. His visitors were gone. He made his humming sounds and pointed when he needed a napkin or wanted to drink. Then, when he had eaten enough, he pointed to the pad of yellow pages. The nurse handed him the pad and pen. He held the pen with care and steadied the pad of paper on his lap. He wrote something and showed it to the nurse. She read it.

"I'll call the church again and see if they know when the priest is coming." She picked up the phone next to his bed and told the switchboard to connect her with St. Vincent's. She didn't have to wait long.

"Hello, I'm Wendell Reese's nurse at Downeast Maine Hospital," she said into the phone. "I wonder when the priest is coming to visit Mr. Reese. He's waiting to meet with the priest." There was a momentary silence as she held the phone to her head. "Thanks, I'll tell him."

She turned to Mr. Reese as she hung up the phone. "He'll be here in two hours."

Mr. Reese smiled, looking pleased. As the tray was removed and his bed put into reclining position, he prepared to rest.

Later in the afternoon, a tall, slender priest came into the room. He was escorted by the nurse who had made the telephone call. They stood in my side of the room and looked at Mr. Reese, asleep in the other bed. I pretended to be asleep in my bed.

The nurse whispered, "I offered to have you meet with Mr. Reese in the chapel, but his daughter thought it would be too hard for him. Can you do it right here? Oh, I should tell you that Mr. Reese can't talk. He can write on his pad, though."

The priest, dignified in a black serge suit and black shirt with white collar, looked somewhat surprised. "Can't talk? I don't know if I can hear a confession in a room like this. It has to be private, of course." Then, thinking a moment, he continued, "The man can't talk; I guess that makes it private."

"Yes, father. It would be private. Mr. Reese has been asking for a priest to hear his confession all day." She whispered, "Plus, he is failing."

The priest nodded his head in understanding as they approached the dying patient on the other side of the room. Mr. Reese woke as the nurse raised his bed. When he was sitting upright, the nurse moved the bedside table so that the old man was comfortable with his pen and the pad of paper. The priest pulled a chair close to Mr. Reese. I could see them silently look at each other, then both men looked at the nurse, who was straightening the bedclothes. She left them, walking to my side of the room. She stopped, and grasping the privacy curtain folded back against the wall, swept it on its overhead rail around my bed, concealing me from them.

I could still hear every rustle of the bedding and puff of air the cushion made when the priest shifted in the chair. Even the noises from the corridor, where lunch trays were being gathered and placed in large stainless steel trolleys, didn't mask the sounds of the two men.

"Your priest, Father Gallagher, is away in Portland. I'm Father Hartley, glad to fill in. Do I understand that you want me to hear your confession?"

I heard the sound of a pen scratching slowly on the paper.

"Oh, I see. You want this to be your final confession. I am sure that Father Gallagher will be disappointed that he can't be here to minister to you, himself. I will do my best for you, indeed I will.

"Confession is very healing, and opening your heart to God will make you feel better. You can write what you want to say to God, through me."

Mr. Reese was writing steadily. The priest responded intermittently with a growing seriousness of tone.

"Did you strike her?"

The sound of the pen at work again.

"Did they fight with weapons?" The priest's voice was now quieter.

The pen scratched an answer as Mr. Reese's gurgling sounds grew louder.

"Are you in this hospital now because she struck you?"

Silence. I could not see whether Mr. Reese was nodding or shaking his head.

"What did you do to show your anger?"

Mr. Reese's humming rose as he replied in writing. I could hear his anguish and emotion even though he was not pronouncing words. The writing was fast and noisy. It sounded like pages flipping quickly.

"Jesus wants forgiveness in your life. You must forgive them, even though they meant you harm…"

I now heard a surge of grunts and attempts to verbalize his anger. The writing was loud.

Father Hartley kept speaking, "…and that by your forgiving them in your family who harmed you, you will help them spiritually. God knows your motives were pure, and forgives you, Mr. Reese."

I clutched the blanket to my throat as I listened. Even though the curtain was closed, I could hear his agitation and feel his anguish.

The nurse suddenly came into my part of the room. She hesitated at the drawn curtain.

"Oh, dear," she whispered. "Mr. Reese's daughter is back." Then to herself, "I'll just have them wait in the waiting room." She glanced at me, and nodded that she would be right back.

My attention turned inward. To me, this is very hard to accept, and I suddenly wished that I could believe that some divine power was watching me and helping me heal, and that I could surrender personal responsibility of my actions and consequences of the factors in my life, so that God would take care of me. I would welcome the comfort of a greater power removing all unknowns and mysteries of my life and the lives I see about me. Wouldn't it be something if the world actually was controlled by a benevolent supreme being that determined every outcome to be just and fair and good? I was weeping because I could not believe in that — although I really wished I could.

There was a pause on the other side of the curtain. I could hear the priest move in his chair. Mr. Reese was now breathing noisily. I could hear him sobbing.

Suddenly, the sound of the pen slowly scratching on the paper resumed.

"Empty-handed, you say? You will not be empty-handed when you enter heaven. The Lord will welcome you to your heavenly home for the good works you have done in your life. You must reflect on the good you have done, and pray that the evil will be banished from your soul by repentance and by your forgiving those who have hurt you.

"The spirit that moves us is divine. Even when we act in ways that cause harm, it's for a reason that God knows. You must do what God moves you to do."

The priest was speaking quietly, calming Mr. Reese with reassuring solemnness.

He continued, "The soul will grow. That is how we learn. It is God's will that you learn and understand why you had to do what you did. God wants there to be forgiveness. Your soul is seeking that forgiveness. God wants you to forgive yourself. Only by forgiving can your soul be at peace, now, and hereafter. This moment, this confession, is when you tell God, through me, his minister, that you see those acts as part of a way to hide your soul no longer. It will be free, then, to join you in its perfect flight from fear. This is God's will and wisdom. This is the treasure your soul brings to heaven."

For a moment it was quiet. The priest was still in his chair. Mr. Reese made no sound. The corridor outside the room was silent.

Father Hartley murmured a farewell to Mr. Reese. Suddenly, the curtain swept back enough for the priest to step through. He stood for a moment looking at Mr. Reese. He pulled the curtain closed, then turned toward the door and strode purposefully out. When he was gone, I clearly heard Mr. Reese crying. The bed creaked as his frail frame shook.

I heard him rip the pages from his pad one by one. Each page he then tore noisily into pieces.

Just then a young nurse I hadn't seen before came to my bedside, pleased to announce that the representative from Guidant had arrived. A tall, beautiful woman, smartly dressed in a tan cashmere suit, strode in carrying a portable computer. To make room for her computer, she stacked the Bible and other book off to one side and rolled the bedside table next to my bed.

"Hi! I'm Ellie. I'm a field engineer for Guidant Corporation, the manufacturer of your defibrillator. Your doctor wanted to be certain that he had turned on your device properly this morning. I can check that out, right now."

She was cheerful and reassuring as she apologized for taking so long to get to the hospital. She had started at four thirty in the morning from Portland, three hours away, and had spent most of the day in Bangor.

"I'm part of the surgery team when a defibrilator is implanted. I usually bring the device from the factory. I also bring the electrical leads that get affixed to the heart muscle. Today, I attended two operations. It's been a long day. I hope they treated you OK here while you were waiting."

She quickly got her computer going, plugged in the donut-shaped wand and placed it on my chest, over my defibrillator.

"This is a magnetic reader that will query your defibrillator's memory. The computer shows what has happened since the last time it was queried. That was five months ago. It looks like it has not had to do anything. Apparently, your heart is getting stronger. Have a look." Ellie turned the screen toward me so I could see a moving electrocardiogram of my own heart. She tapped a few on-screen buttons which instantly revealed that my defibrillator was, in fact, turned on correctly. "Everything is functioning perfectly," she proclaimed.

Ellie expressed such an air of confidence in these devices — she told me it's like having my own personal air bag — that I immediately felt a sense of comfort and assurance. She examined the implant site on my chest. "It looks just as it should," she smiled. This was reassuring. I had worried that the unit might slide about inside my chest.

"You can get up and get dressed. I'll tell the nurse to get your release papers ready. You are fine."

She left me feeling so much better, in part because of her sunny disposition and authoritative knowledge.

Before I left the hospital room some few moments later, I looked over at Mr. Reese. His daughter was lounging in the chair, reading her magazine. Mr. Reese was lying shrivelled in his bed, looking weak and depleted. Shreds of yellow notebook paper were on the floor. He didn't notice me, and I left without saying goodbye.

I would like to thank Janet King for invaluable assistance in the telling of this story.

The B & O, the Circus and Eight Buicks

Sandy Cohen

O n a sunny autumn afternoon, while I was managing my father's broom factory, a thundering, crashing sound and accompanying tremor quaked through the entire brick building. Beyond the shocking sounds, that were so loud they must have come from nearby, there came the simultaneous shaking of the large windows rattling throughout the four story structure. The noise and movement startled the workers, who reacted at the same instant by grabbing onto some fixture or heavy piece of equipment to steady themselves and feel the immediate reassurance of unquestioned immobility. We all looked around in confusion, and in unison formed the same question, "What the heck was that?"

Louie Wink, the foreman and master broom winder at Portage Broom and Brush, turned off his winding machine. Other machines were turned off: the large sewing machines, handle-turning lathes, and broom corn sorting machines, with their noisy shaking bins, also stopped. The entire factory became strangely silent.

Rubbing their hands on their aprons, broom makers throughout the factory grouped at the elevator shaft of their respective floor, shouting to each other the single question, "What the heck was that?"

I went to the office on the ground floor to ask Betty Miller, the office manager what she might know. I could tell by Betty's look of utter bewilderment that she knew no more than anyone else. "Could you call somebody, please, and see what you can find out?"

"I'll call the *Beacon Journal*, maybe they know." She suddenly had another thought, "No, I'll call WAKR." It was the local radio station she listened to. She dialed the number and posed her question to the receptionist. "They don't know anything," Betty said, hanging up.

I climbed the stairs to each floor to make sure that everybody was all right. I looked for damage to the walls, the windows, the pipes and overhead beams and supports. Everything looked intact. I heard a toilet flush, so I assumed that the water system was still working. The lights were still on.

I made an announcement on the public address system, "OK, everybody. Go back to work. I'll investigate what has happened and tell you as soon as I can."

The machines resumed operation, the elevator returned to service and the conversations, shouted over the usual din, speculated whether or not an atomic bomb had just gone off.

I went out the front door and onto Main Street, trying to gather some sensory impressions to lessen the mystery. Off in the distance I heard a police siren with its intermittent shriek. Then, a second siren, the continuous wail of a fire engine. A third siren – I guessed an ambulance – joined, with more sirens, each getting louder, and, I supposed, nearer.

Before going back inside, I noticed a man staggering up the street. He was holding his arm, which was bloody. I approached him and helped him come inside and sit on the wooden bench near our front door. He crumpled onto it like a pile of laundry.

"Are you OK?" I asked.

The stricken man said only one word, "Water."

I got a paper cup of water from the water cooler by the door and handed it to him. He took it with his good hand and drank eagerly, spilling some down his unshaven chin and onto his clothes. His injured arm rested in his lap, but he winced when he moved his shoulder as he drank.

I ran back to the office and told Betty and Cheryl to bring the first-aid kit. Then, I returned to the man.

"We heard a mighty crash. What happened?" I asked.

The man did not speak. He looked at me, but uttered no words. Suddenly, he grasped his bleeding arm and tried to move it to a more comfortable position.

Betty and Cheryl hurried from the office with the first aid kit. They looked at his arm and then at each other, "What could have happened?"

"I don't yet know what happened. But I better get this man to the hospital. He looks pretty hurt. I'll let you know as soon as I can."

The man stood up, rather unsteadily, and I led him to my car. I drove straight to St. Thomas, the nearest hospital emergency room. A young white-coated resident had him lie on a gurney. He examined a wound on the man's leg, pulled off the man's soft-soled pumps and stuffed them under the mattress. The intern then wheeled the patient away. The emergency room started to get crowded with other people. One woman wearing a sequined bathing suit was carried in by a very large man in a cave-man costume.

From various spontaneous conversations sprouting in the waiting area, I learned that a train wreck had occurred somewhere on the Baltimore and Ohio mainline. Those tracks run right next to our factory.

Before the injured man walked out limping, his arm in a sling, I had phoned the office and told Betty what I learned. I offered the man a lift back to where I found him, which he accepted. The doctor approached us at the exit. "Those wounds need time to heal. Try to keep them clean," he told the man. To me, he said, "His leg has been mauled, you know and I gave him a tetanus shot. I also gave him an antibiotic, so he'll need some rest. The forearm is broken. I splinted it, and it should heal in six weeks. The man is healthy, otherwise. Tell him to bathe more often."

"This fellow just stumbled into our factory, doctor. I simply brought him to the emergency room."

In the car, the man started to talk.

"You know Ringling Brothers Barnum and Bailey Circus? I am Tohar, the Alligator Man. The circus train crashed. It must have hit something on the tracks. I don't know. I was in the Pullman. Many people screamed. When everything stopped, I got to the animal wagon. My Delilah was loose. I tried to put the rope on her, she bit my leg." He tried to look at his leg, but couldn't move much in the car seat.

He continued, "Look at my arm. I broke it when the Pullman rolled over. Samson was still in his box. I couldn't get Delilah to hers so I just tied her with the rope to the rail. She's OK. Just scared. Everybody was scared. Samson. Everybody."

Tohar seemed confused. He shook his head from side to side, as if the quick movements would tune in some clear signal of memory.

"I don't know. We go now to play four days in Cleveland. This morning we left Pittsburgh. Sold-out every show. My act is alligators, Samson and Delilah. We get loud applause every time. People love alligators. Anybody can stick his head in alligator jaw; trick is to get it out."

He took a breath as he looked out the window. Traffic was moving slowly. There were police at the bigger intersections, directing cars on.

Tohar, The Alligator Man, resumed, "The Pullman rolled over on its side. That's when Delilah broke free. She never would hurt me, but she was that afraid. Everybody was afraid. She'll be OK."

As he told me this, he started to cry. He put his head in his free palm, and sobbed. I glanced over at him. A man in his late thirties, his black curly hair was long and unkempt, crowding his ears and face. Tohar's face was dark, his eyes black, with bushy brows. The tanned, weathered lines of his face suggested a farmer or sailor. His face was pocked and scarred with numerous cuts, evidence of an eventful history. I guessed he was a Gypsy. He was wearing a tight, torn, and soiled, green T-shirt. His pants were green, too, a loose velour velvet, with a gold sash as a belt. He wore the run down flat-soled, soft slippers that the intern had pulled off in the hospital. Another thing I remember was the smell; a very strong stable smell of straw and manure clung to his clothes and hair. The entire effect of his appearance, which was very unusual to me when I first saw him staggering toward me, now made sense.

As I drove back to the factory, Tohar, the Alligator Man, sat silent, lost in thought. Main Street was now jammed with traffic. A police officer stopped me as I tried to turn at the factory.

"I'm coming from the hospital with this victim off the train. He has to get back to his animals."

The policeman waved us through a barrier that led to the wreck.

The massive steam locomotive and tender were both on their sides. They had rolled onto a parking lot next to the track, crushing several new cars. Steam was still rising from the locomotive. The Baltimore and Ohio livery marking the engine was scraped, scratched and twisted over the tops and hoods of the flattened autos. Many circus train cars, painted with red and gold decorations were strewn over the tracks like a broken accordion. Some train cars were on their sides, some upright, and one upside down.

People crawled over the wreckage. Fire trucks and firemen with their black and yellow coats and helmets worked on the site and people with various injuries lay on the sidelines, being treated and bandaged. Two massive elephants, with harnesses and heavy chains, slowly towed one of the Pullman train cars off the tracks, away from the parking lot area. They were being led by a slight, pretty young woman in a fleece vest. She spoke softly as a poet to them, prodding their ears expertly with a long steel rod.

"There," Tohar pointed to one of the caged animal cars that was on its side.

I steered my car as close as I could. Tohar opened the car door and jumped out. "Later I'll come to say thanks. Now I must find Samson and Delilah."

I returned to the broom factory and told the workers what had happened. They wanted to see the train wreck site. So I gave each person a number 8 warehouse broom (our heaviest) to help clean the disaster area. They all walked together to the site, only a block away.

I phoned my dad, who was at a broom corn auction in Matoon, Illinois, and relayed the story. Indeed, he was very interested, and in particular, he wanted to know about where on the parking lot the train cars had rolled. "I think Tom Botzum owns that lot, and if I'm not mistaken, Sidney Smith at Summit Buick stores his inventory of new Buicks there. I'm gonna call him."

My dad called back fifteen minutes later. "Those were brand new Buick Roadmasters that got flattened by the locomotive. Sidney is insured, so he let me buy eight of them for next to nothing. Go over there and find them, I'll give you the identification numbers. Then call me right away and tell me if they are salvageable. I'm gonna call Buzzy Furst and see if he wants some of them for his junk yard. See if there is one you want. Let me know if there are any convertibles."

Tohar came to the factory the next day. He was limping on his injured leg, and his arm was out of the sling, but still in a cast that was already gray with stains. He had the same dirty, bloody shirt, but was now wearing a pair of faded blue jeans and frayed tennis shoes. He thanked me for helping him, and gave me a front row ticket, marked VIP, for all of the broom factory employees to come to Friday's performance. A mere derailment would not delay the Greatest Show on Earth.

My dad returned the next day. He immediately wanted to see the Buicks. Four he sold to the junk yard, and one that was driveable, he sold to Henry Washington, one of the broom makers on the third floor. Three remaining Roadmasters could be fixed and sold for plenty. There were no convertibles.

All of us from Portage Broom went to the circus together. At the entrance to the big top, Emmitt Kelly, the famous clown, greeted us and ushered us to front row, center ring seats. He tripped twice on the way, and spilled a bucket of confetti on Cheryl. He gave Betty Miller a large cornflower made of crepe paper in a mock act of romantic affection. During the show, other clowns came over to Betty and attempted to water the flower, clumsily throwing buckets of confetti on everybody around. When it was time for Tohar, the Alligator Man, the ring master in his red serge jacket and shiny top hat, announced, with a deep bow and grand wave of his arm in our direction, "Ladies and gentlemen and children of all ages. Ringling Brothers and Barnum and Bailey Circus extends a very special thanks to the folks of Portage Broom and Brush Company, who helped clean up after the train wreck. And for taking Tohar, the Alligator Man, to the hospital.

"And now on with the show."

Tohar came out with two giant alligators on heavy leashes and walked slowly around the center ring. These creatures were amazing to see because of their ferocious appearance and dangerous long teeth and whipping tails. Their yellow eyes peered menacingly at the audience. When he passed us in our seats, Tohar got on top of the alligators, with one foot on each, and they both raised up on their extended legs, and Tohar waved to us and bowed. The audience seemed thrilled by this and clapped their hands enthusiastically. Tohar led Samson and Delilah to the center ring and had them climb over large green barrels and large yellow cubes. Tohar directed Samson to open his vast mouth, which seemed as large as the hood of a Roadmaster! Tohar, the Alligator Man, stuck his entire head into the alligator's fearsome jaws. The band was playing a slow, dramatic drum roll, and the crowd was silent. Even the team of prancing ponies in ring one stopped to watch, as did the clown car in ring three.

Samson seemed to slowly close his mouth over Tohar, and all we could see was the poor man's neck, and his cast-bound arm waving in mock terror. Then, like a slow motion scene, the jaws finally parted and Tohar retracted his head and smiled and stood upright and tossed Samson a fish from a pail on the ground. The crowd excitedly shouted delight and clapped and whistled as the band struck up a lively march, "Entrance of the Gladiators." I breathed a sigh of relief. Tohar bowed. He motioned toward Delilah indicating with hand gestures that she was still shaky after the train wreck. She didn't do anything except look gruesome.

The Visitor

Jean Davison

"GOD!" She says it like she's just discovered a murder in the family. Juliet is curled up in a mountain of pillows in the corner of the front window seat overlooking the ancient spruces that ring my deck. A copy of "The Saga of Dog Island Point," my father's family history of how we came to settle in Maine, lies open in her lap. The saga begins in 1908 when my grandparents took a trip with close friends on one of the lumber schooners that plied the Maine coast. Sailing into Penobscot Bay, they fell in love with Cape Rosier, a broad spit of land named for an early French fur trader. The following year, the two families bought adjacent pieces of property on the cape for $100 an acre.

I can't figure out what would bring such an outburst from Juliet in perusing my Dad's story; I often give it to visitors as a way of introducing them to the place our extended family shares. Maybe it was the price of the land, or perhaps one of the old photographs of people hauling boulders from the bay for the foundation of the original house. Who knows? For the two days since she arrived from California, Juliet has been in high gear, eager to see and do everything – at once.

"What?" I ask her now, nearly cutting my finger along with the tomatoes I'm slicing for lunch. I thought Juliet would enjoy the saga as others have.

"It's so … so … snooty … so class conscious. It's all about names, like Harvard … Smith … the Van Blacks … the Adams … the Emersons."

"I never really noticed, Juliet. This is New England, and I suppose it is more class conscious than the West, more aware of families that go way back. Have you ever heard of the 'Boston Brahmins'? My Dad's parents were from Boston, and most of my cousins and half my siblings live in and around the city."

"Vaguely, but I thought they were a figment of somebody's imagination."

"They were Harvard-educated, first families. Some Bostonians still take this kind of thing seriously. I think my Dad did, to a certain extent. The Emersons were definitely not among the Brahmins, except for someone on my grandmother's side who wasn't a very savory person. But the name evokes a tradition of self-reliance and independent thinking we feel connected to, justified or not. My grandfather used to tell us he could remember sitting on Ralph Waldo's knee as a small child." I laugh to myself. "Whether it was true or not, who cares. I like being connected to the Emersons I know. They're pretty down-to-earth people."

What am I doing trying to defend my Dad's story; my family? But I'm pissed off by Juliet's comments. Maybe it's partly the way she's moved into my house and asserted her will over my space — like the kitchen. She rearranged my cooking utensils and put the coffee maker in another spot the second day she was here. "Hey, I like the coffee maker where it is!" I told her. She frowned. I've bitten my tongue on the utensils.

"Do you want to go mushroom hunting now or after lunch?" I try and deflect my negative feelings toward positive action. Perhaps a walk will help.

"Let's go now. It's still a little misty but the light might be interesting. I'll get my cameras." She heads upstairs to the loft while I put the tomatoes in the fridge.

Juliet and I met through a women's networking group in California and discovered we both like music. She plays the violin. I play piano. She was with the Marin Symphony at the time. I played for myself. We began practicing once a week. She brought the music, and I supplied the wine. Since the late eighties our paths, both marital and professional, have diverged, but our appetite for music and fun has sustained a friendship challenged by distance. This is the first time we've spent a whole week together, living under the same roof.

Juliet is a professional photographer. She specializes in what she calls boudoir photography – a lot of skin, few encumbering clothes. I like what she does, the way she zeros in on shapes and forms, an armpit, the curve of a thigh, legs entwined.

Armed now with a heavy camera bag and tripod, Juliet is ready for our walk in the Maine woods. She looks overburdened. I'll be damned if I'll offer to help. She'd ask if she needed it.

"Here, let me carry the tripod," I hear myself say.

"Okay. That would help."

We follow a steep path down through the woods to the main camp where our communal family's rustic cabins cluster around the original house. Carpets of emerald moss, with an occasional rock poking through, hush our descent. The Big House, as we've called it forever, is a brown-shingled semi-Victorian with a broad front porch running its length and brown shingled wings that jut out on either side. From a distance it resembles a large, oversized hen, wings spread to guard her brood against foul weather on Penobscot Bay. Standing on the front porch, I try and pick out Pumpkin Island lighthouse flattened against Little Deer Isle. Skeins of fog hover above the water, muting distant islands.

"So this is the house that started it all?" Juliet has turned away from the bay. She's looking at the old red and green nautical lanterns that hang on either side of the front door. They're slowly rusting with age and salt.

"Yes. This is the Big House. Do you want to see inside? My sister and her daughters are using it now, but they won't mind if we take a peak at the living room. It's the heart of the place."

"Sure."

I jiggle the handle of the glass-paned front door and push against it. It reluctantly gives way and we go inside. The umber-brown wicker furniture is the original bought in 1918. It includes a long sofa that faces a huge brick fireplace. Juliet stands behind the sofa, taking in the large room. A well-worn log bench sits in front of the hearth. I can smell the ashes of last night's fire. Above the oak mantle, on a shelf in the brick chimney, is a weather worn brass clock that has long since given up on time. Blackened silver trophy cups sit in niches on either side. An old-fashioned life preserver hangs above it. Small triangular sailing flags, faded red and navy blue, hang from the high molding that separates the roof from the room's unfinished walls. The flags bear witness to various family members' placements in past sailing races on the bay. The dates on them go back to the 1920s. Their patriotic colors give the room a slightly festive, if worn, look.

Bookshelves cover the lower part of one unfinished wall. On the other side is a built in desk and an ancient upright piano. The Big House was built before bridges, telephones, and electricity linked people around the bay. There was no electricity until the mid-1950s. The fireplace still provides the main source of heat on cold days.

"My gosh," Juliet exclaims. "This place smells of history. The furniture is even arranged the same way it was in the old photograph I saw in your father's story of the Point. What a great fireplace! Does anyone use the loft? I can see stairs leading up to it, but they look awfully steep and narrow."

"No. Mostly it's used for storage — for sails, old chairs, lanterns, bedding that is stored in a huge chest for the winter, and kids' things. Kids like playing up there, spying on the adults below. One of my nieces' cats hid up there for two weeks before we discovered her."

"What about the piano? Does anyone play it? It almost looks like a player piano with its front panel gone."

"Yeah. My son Rick plays when he comes in July … and one of my nieces. We could have played if you'd brought your violin, but I'm rusty these days."

"I haven't played much either." She's thoughtful for a moment. "This really is a house to be treasured," she says.

The tension I felt earlier over Juliet's remarks about "The Saga of Dog Island Point" begins to dissipate. Perhaps I was being overly sensitive because other things about her had begun to nag me, especially her assertive, take-charge behavior in my house. It was not a side of her I'd seen previously.

Juliet and I leave the Big House and move on across a broad lawn, past a small hillside cottage, to a path through the woods. Our eyes are on the mossy terrain in front of us, seeking out unusual lichen and mushrooms.

"I can see now why you like living here for part of the year … even when it's foggy." Juliet stops abruptly. "Look at these." She crouches to examine translucent white stems thrusting up from a dense forest of moss. Each long stem has a tiny scalloped bulb at the top. "What are they?"

"I have no idea. They're so fragile…like something from another planet. I don't even know if they're mushrooms."

"God, I wish the light weren't so bad. I'd love to take them, but there's no contrast."

"Maybe it will clear a little … it looks like it's trying to."

Juliet has already moved on, examining every stump and clump of moss. "Jeez, look at the size of that mushroom." She points to a large rust red mushroom in the arms of a cedar's spreading roots. Something has eaten away part of its canopy, exposing the white spongy flesh underneath. "Too bad something got to it before we did."

"We'll find more. With all this fog, the mushrooms have taken off."

Juliet wears a white scoop-necked T-shirt, showing appreciable cleavage, tight Capri jeans, and funky tennis shoes. Her honey blond hair is hidden under a broad-brimmed straw hat. She turns back, her oversized glasses perched on her nose. "Remember when we took those 'shrooms before we played music that time?" she asks.

"How could I forget? We were really tripping."

"It was hard to play any music after that."

We continue walking in silence, negotiating the slippery rocks and moss on the trail until we emerge onto a rutted dirt road.

"There's a great shot." Juliet leaves the road and nods toward a cluster of bright orange, delicately fluted mushrooms shaped like moths' wings at the top. They stand out against a cover of wet brown birch leaves and dried spruce tips. Juliet unloads her camera bag and takes out an old battered Nikon. She changes the lens on it. "I wish I had my macro lens and a smaller tripod."

"Can you put the camera on a log?"

"Maybe." She scoots down onto her belly in the wet moss and leaves. "This is the only way to get good shots at this level."

She wallows into the damp earth in front of the mushrooms. I lean the tripod against a rotting stump covered with lichen and squat down behind her. She bends her camera bag and puts it down in front of her, at eye level, then balances her camera on it. "I wish I had a bean bag," she mutters. "It's perfect for close-up shots. You can shape it for just the right angle."

I watch a red-tailed squirrel skittering across a craggy rock, chattering angrily at being disturbed.

"Here goes. Let's hope it works." Juliet presses her eye to the lens, then moves the camera a fraction to the right. She takes the shot. Another one follows from a slightly different angle. "The light's getting better," she says, looking around at me from her prone position.

I get down on my belly, too, inhaling the slightly acrid smell of molding leaves around me. "This is kind of fun, Juliet." I'm scanning the forest floor for other mushrooms. To my left are tiny convex ochre-brown mushrooms, one slightly larger than the other, protruding from the base of a torn fir stump. It's like a Japanese miniature, perfect in every detail.

"Hey Juliet. I've found another."

"Where?" She gets up from her cramped position.

Her Clorox-white T-shirt is covered with slimy mud. She holds it out from her body, looking at it. "This is what I don't like about this kind of photography."

I nod and point to the mushroom vignette I've discovered.

"That is a beauty." She wiggles down on to her stomach again, and positions the Nikon on her bag, while I kneel next to her.

She's in the middle of the shot when one of my sixty-something cousins, Jody, and her daughter come along the road in my cousin's red Subaru. Jody stops and studies us for a moment, concern etching her face. "Are you okay?"

"Yes," I smile. "We're photographing mushrooms; they're great this year. This is my friend, Juliet."

My cousin's worried look changes to relief. "Hello," she greets Juliet with an amused grin as she watches her hoisting herself into a standing position.

"Hi," Juliet says, coming to the edge of the road with her camera.

"This is my cousin Jody, and her daughter, Karen."

"Nice to meet you." Juliet eyes my dark-eyed, curly haired cousin with a mixture of embarrassment and curiosity. I can tell she is not what Juliet expected; neither is her perky daughter. Both are dressed in worn T-shirts and khaki shorts.

"For a minute we thought you'd had a heart attack … or something," Jody says.

Juliet giggles. "Sorry we gave you a scare. Just doing some wet belly photography," she explains. "It's messy, but the results, if they come out, are worth it."

Jody glances at Juliet's T-shirt. "I see what you mean." She laughs. "Well have a good time and if you're down near the Gray House, stop by."

"Thanks." Juliet sounds pleased.

Starting the car again, Jody and Karen wave as they take off.

"What a lovely smile," Juliet says. "I like your cousin. Where does she live when she's not in Maine?"

"In Woburn, a blue-collar town north of Boston. She's a social worker."

"Really? Guess she's not sitting around on her Brahmin behind."

"Well, like I said, even though my father's generation may have been into social class, things have changed. I notice it, especially, among my kids' generation. Economically, there's a broader spread, and more regional and ethnic diversity. They've intermarried more than our generation, and live in states further away. One lives in Taiwan. But when all the cousins, second cousins, and those once removed, get together here nothing seems to matter except preserving the feeling of this special spot for future generations. I like the changes, the diversity. It enriches the family."

"I see what you mean – as varied as the mushrooms we saw today. When I get my pictures developed, I'll send you copies."

Three weeks after Juliet leaves, I get a fat, brown package from her. Inside are black and white photos she took of Blue Hill and Deer Isle, and in color, shots of Buck's Harbor, Dog Island Point, and her close-ups of mushrooms and lichen. The mushroom vignettes are my favorite, exquisite in detail and lighting. Their beauty makes me realize why, after all, I value Juliet's friendship. She's a true artist, not afraid of getting down in the mud.

Kenny and Loretta

Maureen Farr

If I hadn't forgotten my lunch, things would have turned out differently. I had to go back to the house to get it, and that's when the trouble began.

You wouldn't think that in the ten minutes since I left, Kenny could have gotten a girl into our bed. But he did. He's like that — a great planner.

I came back into the kitchen and there was the brown bag with my lunch in it right where I left it on the table. And there was a pair of ladies' heels on the floor. They weren't mine and they sure as hell weren't Kenny's. They were black, high-heeled jobs with silver trim around the ankles. I slipped off my right shoe and put my foot into one of them. It must have been a size ten, and it really wasn't my style. I go for the more comfortable type — you know, like Birkies.

There was a trail of clothing leading to our bedroom door — a red dress, black panties, black slip, ending with a pair of black nylons. None of them were mine either. I thought I saw Kenny's shirt in there somewhere.

I picked up the dress and held it in front of me. I ran my hands over it, feeling the contours of my body through the washed silk. I caught my reflection in the kitchen window, and thought I'd look pretty damn good in the thing.

There was a loud shriek from the bedroom as the door burst open and this Amazon of a girl came running out into the hallway. She was naked except for a black lace bra. It was a pushup type, but it wasn't pushing up much of anything.

She was laughing, but she stopped as soon as she saw me, and put her hand to her mouth. She whispered softly, "Oh shit!" Just like that — like I was the one who wasn't supposed to be there.

I felt like an idiot, standing there with my right foot in her high heel. I started to explain that I forgot my lunch and came back and saw the shoes on the floor. "I just tried one on, you know?" My face got hotter and hotter with every word. "Um … is Kenny in there?" I pointed to the bedroom.

She nodded wordlessly as I handed her the red dress. As she tried to cover up and back away from me, Kenny came out of the bedroom. Except for his cowboy boots and a Stetson, he was naked, too. He had a little leather whip in his right hand.

The Stetson was too big, and it bent his ears over so he looked like a puppy with a hat on. Kenny is self-conscious about the size of his ears — they're pretty small for such a tall guy. I thought he'd be embarrassed if he looked in the mirror. Right at that moment, everything about Kenny looked pretty small.

"Aw, fuck," he said when he saw me. "What the hell are you doing here? I thought you went to work." He looked down at my foot in the size ten high-heel.

I realized how stupid it all was — me standing there with one black high-heel and one brown Birkie on, and those two mostly naked. Not as stupid as Kenny looks in that Stetson, I thought.

I slipped my foot out of the girl's shoe and back into my own Birkie. Picking up my lunch I blurted, "I forgot this." I could see the girl out of the corner of my eye gathering up the rest of her clothes as she backed into the bedroom. I figured she'd put them on and get, so I stood where I was and looked Kenny in the eye.

"What the hell are you doing?"

He just glared at me like I was the one who did wrong.

We stood like that — me looking him in the eye, and him glaring at me — for maybe a minute. "Well," I said, "if you don't have an answer, I guess I'll go to work. I hope Miss High-Heels is gone before I get back … You too," I said just before I closed the door behind me. I had gone down half a flight of stairs when the door opened again and she emerged, looking flustered and angry.

"I'm really sorry," she offered as she caught up to me on the stairs. "He said it was over between you two or I never would have come here."

"Why would any guy invite you over in the morning for chrissake?" I asked. She shook her head.

"Some date," I said continuing down the stairs.

"Hey!" Kenny leaned over the banister above us. "Don't go. I can explain." We both kept moving down the stairs. If I feel stupid, what about her?

He kept shouting as we went downstairs. "Please! I can explain. Don't go!" Finally, we heard the apartment door slam two flights up.

At the second floor, she grabbed my arm. "Please let me explain."

"No need," I replied.

At the first floor, "I'm sorry," again.

"It doesn't matter. He's right — it is over between us, but it's not your fault."

When we got out on the street, she turned uptown as I headed downtown. I took a couple of steps, turned and looked at her walking in the other direction.

Damn, she looked good in that red dress.

Unkindness of Ravens

Maureen Farr

My old man died on the first day of autumn. It wasn't exactly unexpected, but still. Right up to the end, he was full of surprises. Like when he knew he was going he washed the stack of dishes in the sink and put them on the drainboard to dry. So Ma said he knew he was going.

"First time in twenty years he done the dishes." That's what Ma said, and I believe her.

But how in hell did he know? Did he know he was going to keel over in the bathroom, hit his head on the sink, and bleed all over the place? Who did he think would get stuck with the job of cleaning it up? Right. Ma — just like always.

If he sensed what was going to happen, wouldn't he have gone straight to bed without washing his teeth?

I asked my Ma that. She just shook her head like I was some kind of nut case or something.

I mean, maybe he would have. If he went straight to bed, when the stroke got him he would have been lying down already, see? So he wouldn't have gone ass over teakettle and hit his head.

"He knew it was coming," Ma said. She thinks that because of him washing up the dishes and all. But I don't think so. I think he would have gone right off to bed. He would have figured the pearly whites didn't matter much where he was headed. Most nights, before he went to bed, he went outside on the back porch and just pissed over the railing into the daylilies.

Some nights, when we were little, he was so stinking drunk that he'd pitch right over that railing. My brother and I would climb out our bedroom windows and watch from the porch roof as Ma went out to help him up.

I used to wonder why she never got mad at him. I mean, here's this deadass drunk pissing into her prized bed of daylilies. The house sits on the curve that looks right over the cove where they moor the lobster boats. Which means if someone drove by at the right time, and their highbeams were on, why, they'd be able to see his pecker.

But Ma would just go out and pull him by the arm. "John," she'd say. "If you can't aim any better than that, maybe you should come back inside and go to bed."

He'd drape his arm over her shoulders and kiss her. He'd almost always start singing, but Ma would shush him. Some nights it was that Patsy Cline song "Walkin' After Midnight." Other times, well, it was something else.

My brother and I would lie on our bellies up there on the porch roof, looking down at the two of them in the moonlight. One night, Pa lifted his head to the heavens and saw us.

"Christ, Evvie," he shouted at Ma. "There's goddam angels up there."

Ma looked up too, put her finger to her lips, and gestured at us to go back inside. "John, I think the drink's gone to your head," she said. "There's nothing up there but the Big Dipper."

The next morning at breakfast, Ma told us she didn't want us out on the porch roof at night. "Why, you could fall into the daylilies along with your Pa, and then I'd have three of you staggering around in your skivvies." I think she just didn't want us to see Pa drunk.

I giggled, but Johnny said, "How come Pa pisses over the railing, Ma? Anybody could see him. It's goddam embarrassing."

My brother was fourteen at the time, so I guess he figured swearing was okay. But Ma just backhanded him. "I'll not have any cussing at my table," was all she said.

Johnny pushed away, sending his chair over backwards to the floor. "Right," he shouted. "No cussing at the table, but Pa can get dead drunk, piss over the goddam porch rail — why, Hell! He can even fall over the damn thing and you just clean up behind him."

He threw the screen door open.

"I've gotta go."

The screen door slammed behind him, and he did.

Ma got up from the table. I remember how she looked when she took his dishes to the sink. I thought sure she was going to cry, and I said, "Did you hear the one about the man who had two left shoes?"

"Don't you think you should get ready for school, young lady?" she asked, as she turned back to the table and took my dish away.

"Ma! I wasn't done," I said, but I knew that as far as she was concerned, I was.

Even after that — Johnny and me — we'd still climb out on that roof and watch when Pa got drunk. Johnny said one night that he thought the reason the daylilies were so orange was because Pa's piss was so full of whiskey.

I was only nine, and I didn't know if that was true or not, but I don't think so. I mean, if whiskey is so good for plants, why not just pour it on them? When I asked Johnny that one, he said I didn't understand science. He told me that your body changes things like whiskey and food into other stuff that's good for you.

"Like what?" I asked him.

"Muscles. Brain cells. Strong bones and stuff—"

I whispered, "Whiskey can do all that?"

"Naw," he answered. "But the food can. We've been learning all about stuff like that in school this week. Do you know what a light year is?"

"Nope," I said. I laid there in the dark, grit from the shingles digging into my bare shoulders, and all those millions of stars over my head listening to Johnny tell me about the constellations and how far away from us they were.

"Space is so big that they measure distance in light years — imagine it! The distance of one light year is so long we can't even live through one." He was so excited, his voice shook.

I rolled over onto my belly and looked down into the yard. Yellow light spilled from the open kitchen door across the grass.

Suddenly, Pa's shadow filled the shaft of light and then he was outside on the edge of the step. The screen door banged and I whispered, "There's Pa!"

We watched as he staggered down the steps into the back yard. "Evvie," he shouted back at the house. "Come on out here and watch the shootin' stars with me. Evvie! Get out here." He tried to sit on the old wooden chair out by the clothesline, missed it and landed flat on his back. Just about that time, my Ma came out on the porch. She saw him fall, muttered something, and rushed to his side.

He pulled her down on top of him and they started fumbling around. He pulled her dress up and I could see her white panties and her nylon stockings that she rolled and knotted above her knees.

I was embarrassed and started to giggle. Johnny cursed.

I guess Ma must have heard us because she made Pa stop. She managed to get her dress pulled down at the same time that she stood up and looked towards the porch roof. By then, we had wiggled back out of sight and were holding our breath.

I could see Johnny's eyes glinting as he looked at me. "Don't move a muscle or we're done for." He whispered so softly I could barely hear him, but I knew I better do what he said.

"Come on inside, John." Ma spoke a little louder than normal, and I thought maybe she was warning us. She got him moving towards the house, and when he went inside she said, "I'm just going to pull the chair onto the porch. I'll be right in." I could hear him mumbling something as he shuffled through to the front stairs.

"If you two scallawags know what's good for you, you'll be in bed and asleep before I get up those stairs to check on you." It sounded like she was right underneath us on the back porch. It was said lightly, but I thought Ma was pretty mad.

We waited 'til we heard her pick up the chair and start back towards the porch, and then we both made a beeline for the window into my room. Johnny gave me a quick kiss on the top of my head and slipped out into the hall. "G'night," he said as the door clicked shut.

I swear it wasn't half a minute before Ma opened that door and came in. I felt the edge of the bed sink under her weight and I pretended to be deep asleep. "I know you're awake," she said in her you've-been-a-bad-girl voice. I breathed deeply, hoping she'd believe I really was asleep.

"How many times have I told you not to go out on the porch roof?"

She sighed, and I felt the shift of her weight.

Then she did the strangest thing. She just started talkin'. Not to me. It was like she was talkin' to God or something.

"Jesus, I don't know what to do. I try my damnedest to bring up these kids right, and then he — Oh hell, what does it matter? I just wish they didn't have to see this. Well, anyway." That was all she said, and then she left. As she closed the door, the light from the hall flitted across my bed in a long, slanty way, and I started crying.

* * *

So when the old man kicked the bucket, I felt like it was justice. I mean, he wasn't the most likable guy in the world. Mostly, he was an ornery man. He didn't have much to say unless it was something like, "Goddam draft dodgers were down to the courthouse again today." " Dick Nixon should just nuke ole Ho Chi Minh and be done with it all."

Pa served in World War II, and he didn't take to anyone who didn't believe in fighting. So that's probably why he took Johnny for a ride on his eighteenth birthday. He drove him down to the draft board to register.

Ma sat at the kitchen table when they left. "Some birthday present that is," she said as she wiped her eyes with her apron and stared out the kitchen window. Johnny's birthday was November fourteenth, but I don't remember it being very cold that year.

He got called up just after Thanksgiving. Ma really cried the night before he left, and begged Pa to drive him to the Canadian border so he wouldn't have to serve. "It's only three hours away," she said. I remember she was sitting in the old rocker by the kitchen stove.

Pa's face turned beet red as he loomed over her. "No son of mine is going to turn tail and run," he said in a low, menacing voice. His hands gripped the arms of the rocker so hard the knuckles turned white. "No sirree, I served in W-W-Two and I'd go tomorrow if they needed me.

"Johnny's going and he's damn proud to be doin' it. Ain't you son?" Johnny just glared at him. I had such a lump in my throat that I couldn't eat my apple pie. Ma made it special because it was Johnny's favorite. Mine, too, but I couldn't choke it down that night to save my soul.

After boot camp, Johnny got to come home for a month before being shipped overseas. By then, it was late February and colder than hell.

He had one of those buzz cuts they give you in the army.

"You cold, with all your hair gone?"

He just looked at me.

"Colder than I've ever been in my whole life, Bug."

That was his nickname for me — short for ladybug because he said when I was born I had all these red spots on my face and my belly.

When he said that about being cold, I got chills. I couldn't figure exactly what he meant, but it scared me something awful. I wanted to hug him, but he wouldn't hear of it.

Early in the morning of the day he left, I woke to the sound of ravens in the yard. There was the rumbling sound of lobster boats down in the cove as they headed out for a day's fishing. It was just coming light, so it must have been about five or six. In the next room, I heard my brother's bed creak as he rolled over and grumbled in his sleep.

I looked outside and there was one raven on the porch roof and another in the old maple tree on the lawn. They were cawing back and forth. Then I heard my mother say, "It's an unkindness."

"What?" Pa asked. He sounded half asleep. They were still in bed, too, across the hall.

"Ravens," she said. "An unkindness of ravens," and I knew then I'd never hear my brother in his room again.

At breakfast, I asked her what an unkindness of ravens was. She didn't answer, just raised her spoonful of oatmeal to her lips.

I guess you're wondering what happened next, right? Johnny came home in a body bag about six months after being shipped out. By then, Pa had started an about-face and decided that war wasn't such a good idea after all. It wasn't the draft dodgers down to the courthouse. Oh, no. He'd been listening to the guys up to the Amvets Hall. Seems, when it hurts your business, war ain't so good after all. I remember Pa saying, "This country can't afford to be fighting someone else's war," and he said it more than once.

He never said we can't afford to lose our boys — it all had to do with business. That was Pa all right. You'd think war wouldn't hurt a lobster fisherman none, but Pa complained bitterly that it had.

The day we buried Johnny, there was ravens in the graveyard. The minister said some words I don't remember, and then came this loud explosion. Those ravens took off squawking and shrieking, but not before three of them lay dead on the ground.

I turned and saw Ma with the shotgun from Pa's truck. "Are you crazy, woman? Someone could of been killed," Pa shouted at her.

"Someone was," she said, and dropped the gun. The church service had been crowded with folks from the town — all the lobstermen and their wives, kids Johnny knew from school, his teachers. They all started leaving the grave-yard, and the minister went to Ma and tried to help her but she shook him off. She marched back to Pa's old, green Ford pickup and got in behind the wheel. She blew the horn, and that huge flock of ravens took off from the trees they had perched in after she fired the shotgun.

"Come on," she shouted to me and Pa. "There's nothing more to be done here. Let's go home." I got in the other side and slid over close to her, and Pa came along with the shotgun. He just shook his head as he got in and slammed the door.

* * *

Yeah, Pa keelin' over like that seems like justice all right. If he hadn't taken him down to the draft board Johnny might still be here. If he was, he'd be forty-nine now. I wonder if he would have lobstered, like Pa. I asked Ma if she thought Johnny would have been fat and bald by now, and she gave me that look.

I'm more than forty myself, been married and divorced, and got a couple of grown kids of my own. Ma can't send me to my room anymore, but I still feel like she can when she gives me that look.

She never talks about Johnny. She hasn't uttered his name since the day we got the news. And then, she just wailed it out one time. After that, she acted like he never was.

I wasn't home when she cleaned out his room. She closed the door, and never opened it again as far as I can tell.

But I went in every now and again. I'd sit on his bed, but it wasn't the same. That's all there was, just the bare mattress. All his stuff was gone.

He used to make these model planes that he hung over his bed and desk. He had a collection of skulls he found in the woods. And his books — I always wondered where they went.

When I moved back home after my divorce, I went into Johnny's room and sat there. I sat there and thought of that morning when I heard the ravens and my brother turning over in his bed. I sat on that bed and I missed him like crazy.

After Pa's funeral, I asked Ma about the unkindness of ravens. "What in hell are you talking about?" she asked.

"I remember you said it the day Johnny went off," I began. "And then, at his funeral, those ravens was there— "

"Hush," she said. "It's a sad day. We don't need to be talking about nothin' like that now."

"But," I began, and she stopped me.

"We've got people coming. Get out in the kitchen and make up some coffee."

There's days when I miss my brother, but I haven't yet had a one where I miss Pa. He wanted to be cremated, his ashes scattered over the sea from a plane. I never knew that 'til after he died, and I asked Ma why.

"He loved the sea. But I'm not going to do it."

She thought she should put him on the daylilies.

"There's a lot of your Pa in those lilies," she said with a small smile.

I got that feeling, like somebody walked on my grave.

"You can't do that," I said. "If he wanted to be scattered on the sea then we have to do it."

"I never liked that damn ocean. I can't swim."

Then she said the only hope was to go up in a plane.

"And I'm not going. I can't go up there. Open the window, and dump him out like that."

"I'll do it," I said.

I can't figure why I said it, because I haven't done a blessed thing Pa wanted me to since the day we buried Johnny. I never could forgive him. I still feel like it was him killed my brother, not some little guy in black pajamas halfway around the world.

I had to call the airport and find out who had a small plane to take me up. It turned out to be Billy Horstman, except now he calls himself Bill. When he found out I was Johnny's sister, he said there'd be no charge. Seems he was "in 'Nam" with Johnny. How come I didn't remember that?

It's strange how one death brings up another one, you know? Pa died on the first day of autumn; Johnny's been gone more than thirty years. I cried for one but I can't cry for the other.

So, on a Sunday two weeks after Pa died, Billy Horstman called me up and said it was a good day for scattering ashes.

"I'm going out to the airport today," I told Ma at breakfast. "At eleven."

"Well, I'll go with you."

"Stay home, Ma. I'm going up in a plane. Billy Horstman's taking me. Remember him? I'm taking Pa's ashes."

We got in a big fight, and the next thing the doorbell was ringing and it was Billy Horstman.

I asked him in and Ma said hello, and isn't it a lovely day? and put her handkerchief to her eyes and turned away. Then Billy did the nicest thing. He put his arm around her and said, "You can talk to me Mrs. Johannson, and I'll listen." And me? I guess I just fell in love with that man right then and there.

I mean, how can you not love a man who'd say that to a grieving widow? It was like Bruce Willis in that movie with Demi Moore, the one where he dies and then comes back and she can't see him? Except I don't think it was Bruce Willis. It's that other guy — Patrick Swazey. Now there's a hunk of a man, and I tell you Billy Horstman reminds me of him. And not just because he was nice to Ma or nothing. He's got that look.

Billy helped her into her sweater and I picked up the box that had Pa in it. It was heavier than I expected and I said, "Pa's put on some weight," which made Ma smile again. We all went out to Billy's truck, a new four-wheel drive that sits up about eight feet off the ground, and Ma couldn't get up there without him helping her. He grabbed hold of her arm with his left hand, put his other hand on her waist, and just sort of lifted her right up into the back seat.

I wanted to seem like a woman who could take care of herself, so I hopped up into that front seat quicker than a cat on a mouse. I swear I saw Billy smile.

When we got to the airport, Billy settled Ma in the "Executive Lounge" where she could watch out the big window and see the planes coming and going. Of course, where we were, it was only the little planes, but she didn't care.

I carried Pa out to the plane, then Billy took the box and opened the door for me. "What do you call this thing?" I asked him, and he looked at me funny and said, "A door." I just thought it would have a different name, like a hatch on a boat. He handed me the box with Pa in it, and closed the door.

I was scared after we took off, but Billy seemed so confident that I almost forgot why we were up there. We flew around for about fifteen minutes, heading out over the Atlantic. It was one of those beautiful blue sky days we get in fall, the ones where the blue hurts your eyes. And those little sheep clouds pop up and float along and then just seem to disappear.

I was lost somewheres far away — woolgathering is what Ma calls it — when Billy spoke, "Remember what I said about when you dump the ashes?" I nodded, but I didn't — not really. He leaned across and slid the window open. "Is this called a window?" I shouted, and he just laughed. I leaned out then, holding that box tight in the wind, afraid I'd drop the whole thing into the sea.

As I tipped the box and poured my father out on the ocean, I thought again of the unkindness of ravens. And then, wouldn't you know? Dammit if Pa's ashes didn't come swirling right back up into my face, and back in the window of that plane. I did drop the box then, but it didn't matter.

"Look out," Billy shouted, and reached past me to close the window. "I told you to dump them low, remember?"

"I guess I forgot," I said as he brushed ashes from my face with his right hand. "We'll have to clean you up before your Ma sees this, or she'll be a goner, too," he said, and we both laughed.

"Do you know about the unkindness of ravens?" I asked him, and he just stared at me.

"Well, do you?"

"Yes, I do," he said.

"Tell me," was all I could answer.

"Alright," he said, and that was that.

April After Ice: Augusta to Belfast

Mile after mile, some blind goddess
Raked the land with icy fingers
Dog-earing trees to mark each
Edge of road, brook, field, and pond
She could feel in her anger but not see.
Where ice did not snap the branches,
It swept off the crowns of trees
To drop them that way and this
Among now naked stumps,
Great spruce arrows pointing skyward
To the source of their agony.
Many trunks were tortured by the added weight,
Turned into tank traps of warning
To any daemon thinking of
Serving up another ice assault.
Here a birch mimes exploded halves
Of Independence Day salutes;
There another leans its frozen arch
Obeisant still to winter's ice.
A large popple seems more vocal,
Its top lying broken, spare,
Its branches like arms reaching from the ground,
Cringing as in pain.
Some trees, maples mostly,
Leave good taste behind,
Their butts raised high, obscene,
A gesture of derision,
But others, split and peeled from top to ground,
Leave great tongues sticking
From the forest in contempt.

In settled stretches
The severed limbs are stacked,
Sometimes six feet up or more,
Broken ends to the streets,

Racked for transport.
Some damage on more rural roads
Is already removed from view,
Cut flush and shredded, the larger chips
Still gleaming gold before they'll bleach out
To gray and disappear into the forest floor.
In other places what were woods are newly bare;
Old walls, long lost, return;
Like aged fading coastal prints,
The dearth of trees evokes surprise.
It makes one think, but choose the context,
A clear cut can be merciful.

Heading east, the setting April sun behind,
The forest holds its wake;
A thousand breaks flame orange,
The trunks like candles in the pre-green spring.

—Hendrik D. Gideonse

Harbor Gift

I live well into the woods
A scant quarter mile as the raven flies
From the tidal flats of Herrick Bay.
I've known for quite some time
That trees sweep water from the fog;
When driving by the shrouded bay
My eyes will see but car lengths beyond my hood,
But moments later at my well-swept
Clearing I plainly see
The blue late season Canterbury bells,
The plumping pink of phlox,
The orange petals embracing all my Susans'
Deepset eyes of brown.

This morning I've seen
The hints of sun behind the glowing fog,
So paint can, brush, and towel in hand
I head for the harbor to stem
A stubborn stain on my lobster cabin ceiling.
I scrub the roof, sluice clean, and towel her off.
With sun now clearly breaking through
I leave the roof to dry
And take the dog to walk.

I please us both by pitching sticks
Far out from shore for Hogan to retrieve,
And when he's done with water play
I stroll the east side of the isle
Beach-combing as I like to do,
My back to the water, eyes roaming
The meandering line of tidal drift.
The now strong morning sun
On Chatto's towering spruces
Reveals they've swept departing fog
Of a million twinkling drops of water
Each one refracting rainbow glints,
A stunning stand of Christmas trees
Sparkling for just a moment before
The lights disappear into thin air
In an August morning's building heat.

—Hendrik D. Gideonse

Porpoises

I first saw porpoises in Long Island Sound,
Long lines of them, parallel to the shore,
Headed west or east at Old Field Beach.
Then later in the Reach
I'd see them from my boat on certain days
When wind was light and water not too broken;
Their glistening backs and dorsal fins
Would slowly break the surface.
They'd breathe, and wheel beneath
To break again some fifty feet away
Though exactly where one could not say.

One time, in irons, adrift, no sound from wind or sails,
A mother and her child played all around my stern,
Her "poosh," its "pish," each breathing
On their easy broaches left and right,
To underscore the image held so long,
Of porpoise gentle, sure, together, pure.

And then late last fall in empty Center Harbor
Standing at the floatless pier I was amazed to see,
In spaces I never imagined they'd be,
A dozen of them, perhaps,
Playing out the chilly setting sun.
The gentle arcs of pairs and threes
Turned slowly here and there,
A twist, a roll, a tag team match at watery play,
Until in the upper corner of my eye
A dorsal fin exploded up
To streak straight as an arrow
Seventy yards or more, unerring,
To a spot just near where my boat
Would have floated had she not been
In her winter shed,
And through that singular and swift event
Augments my slow-grown images of gentleness and play
With proof of brutish power and violent intent.

—Hendrik D. Gideonse

An Existential Moment Slow to Come

Spring this year was slug-like,
An interminable overture
To the longed-for music of summer.
The first nubs of April green,
Tipped yellow from the many mid-spring freezes,
Didn't push their way through mulch and mud
Until mid-month, and even then
The upward thrusts proved snail-like, too —
An eighth inch a day,
Sometimes a quarter,
And sometimes none.
One day, though, they grew an inch,
The next another, and then a third,
But the skinny slips of buds
Proved faint of promise
Wraith-like as they were.
By April 20th they'd reached their proper height
But stood, still thin,
And proudly straight without a hint of
Dipping down to proper tilt for daffodils.
The 21st brought a little sign of letting go,
The next day a clear incline to one o'clock,
The next at two, the fourth at three.
The tips fattened as temperatures hit seventy,
And still the buds held back,
But on the 28th the first trumpet
Blared out its golden sound,
And the very next day the entire brass
Ensemble poured forth its joy,
As Baba Ram Dass would say,
At being here now — at last.

—Hendrik D. Gideonse

Backstairs

Brenda Gilchrist

At the end of June, I carry all my work papers and reference books, computer and printer; files of unpaid bills and Met Opera folder; tins of muchi curry powder and cumin, bottles of Thai peanut satay, Szechuan spicy stir fry, and garlic tamari sauce; summer cotton T-shirts, flowered rayon skirt, and linen Flax pants in the garden cart from my big house on Deer Isle to the Trivet, a small cabin on the shore a hundred feet away, where I spend my summers in petulance and obsequiousness.

For the past several years, I've been renting my house, which — just so you know — was designed in 1902 by Alexander Wadsworth Longfellow, Henry Wadsworth's nephew, for another uncle of his, James Croswell, also my great-uncle, whose wife, Leta, my great-aunt, left it to her niece, my aunt Eleanor, who left it to me.

Bracey, my Welsh corgi, whose lineage, by the by, can be traced back to twelfth-century Flanders, doesn't share my peevish frame of mind, but remains at his command post outside the front door of the house during my move to the cabin. He sometimes takes up this position even after the move, if he feels guests at the big house need to be greeted.

At first, the Trivet is delightful; life is simplified by the small space, and I like to hear the waves move on the beach at night and the eider ducks talk in the morning. At breakfast, I bring my mug of coffee onto the tiny screened porch and look across the bay to the Camden Hills, observing the mist opening and shutting the view, Hard Head and Butter islands etherializing into blue, streaming vapors, shifting from substance to dreams. I am lucky to be here on this isolated point of land, I think.

Then I hear voices on the other screened porch at the big house, cups and plates — the inexpensive Corelle ware, I hope, not the Quimper or Worcester — clattering on the green painted table. I can't even console myself for my reduced circumstances by imagining that I am a rusticator on an undiscovered Down East shore.

Also, that screened porch is bigger than mine. The tenants are more convivial, sociable — and far, far wealthier. I can hear them talk about weekends in Budapest, freighter trips around the Horn, treks in Nepal. I have to rely on their providence to supply me with income to live, on the bountifulness of those people sitting on the big porch, my superiors, bosses, isolationists, antiaffirmative action Republicans, fascists, Nazis.

What upsets me particularly is when Bracey and I take our evening stroll around the confined circumference of the Trivet and I can see them eating dinner downstairs while all the bedroom lights are blazing upstairs. The house looks like the *Titanic* going down, Bracey and I in a lifeboat looking across the black water. I want to go over there and tell them: For Christ's sake, turn the lights off upstairs! I don't, of course. Bracey would do it, but I can't ask him.

One morning, I tap on the glass front door of the big house and wait, hand to forelock, for someone to come. Bracey is preoccupied with crows searching for leftover birdseed under the bird feeder.

"What can we do for you?" she says brightly, holding the door open. "Come in, come in!" She is dressed in navy blue shorts and a white polo shirt, tucked in.

How good she is, I think. Imagine inviting me into this large, clean house. I shall surely muck it up.

"I just want to get a file from my office. I hate to bother you. I'll rush up the backstairs. I won't take a minute. I'll be out of here in a flash."

Don't look at me, I think. Don't watch as I run across your shining white pine floors and up your backstairs to my office, to what used to be the maid's room, with its own backstairs, shut off from the rest of the house. The family always employed the front stairs with the thin, elegant Arts and Crafts banister and balustrades; the backstairs are suitable for me.

"I'll only be a minute, I promise."

I won't damage anything, I think of adding. I'll try not to knock over the flowered Bavarian teapot or the green Moustier bowl or the round platters with Quimper peasant women. I'll duck around the corner to the stairs and you won't even know I've been here.

I must be careful, not make a habit of coming over here, might want some of the things these spoiled, rich people have. Look at that marble top, inlaid chest, on which my distant step-cousin Harriet Beecher Stowe wrote, at the foot of the stairs. No, don't take the time. I'll be distracted by things, become like them. Run up the stairs and get the file on the Penobscot Bay Turtles Investors Club.

Breaking in, that's what I'm doing — well, not exactly, the owner is standing in the hall, she let me in, she isn't the owner anyway — to get a folder on learning how to buy stocks: I, the poor relation! the paid gardener!

I am like them. I am them. I am the owner. I own this mansion with the Louis XV inlaid table with cabriole legs and hoof feet. The Quimper platters are mine. The marbletop chest is mine.

Bracey remains at his post by the front door. The activities of black ants in the grass interest him. He has no problems with self-pity, has not altered his personality, has kept his personhood. Mine is in jeopardy.

I rush down the backstairs and out the door with my file.

"Thanks! Thanks! I have my file. I am so grateful to you. What a lovely house."

Stop this. I am breathless when I get back to the Trivet. Bracey waits at the big house, he doesn't follow me back. He knows his place is there, as it is here, wherever he is.

On the Trivet screened porch I drink another mug of coffee, quiet my knocking chest.

Ask yourself, I say to myself. Who is the owner of that big house one hundred feet from here?

Is it the woman in the navy blue shorts and tucked-in, white polo shirt or is it I, sitting at the dining table, whipping the tenants with the straw placemats, holding the ends with my two hands and flapping them at their faces, leaving woven marks on their cheeks, yelling, "Turn off the lights upstairs! Do it right now. Up the stairs you go! Pronto!"?

The tenants scrabble up the backstairs, wailing and nervous. I see all this from my little porch in the Trivet.

Morpho Nimbus

Brenda Gilchrist

She walks in the door carrying a bunch of lamb's ears.

"I must put them in water immediately," she says.

Her hair, fluffed out against the stars, cumulus around her head, fills the doorway.

Is this a hostess present, I wonder?

"Please show me where I can put them," she says, importantly.

Dressed in silky white pants and an abbreviated black tanktop, she is the essence of professional New York, of Madison Avenue art director, gold rings and bracelets gleaming on her hands and wrist.

Bracey greets her loudly in the small mudroom. His round, cylindrical body wriggles with enthusiasm; he misses New York.

I locate a large, crystal vase for the thick, gray, hairy lamb's ears, which she places in the hallway.

"They will be all right here," she says.

I guess they're not for me.

At dinner, she feeds Bracey pieces of roast chicken and kernels of yellow and white corn.

Eyes riveted on her face and hands, body rigidly expectant, his whole world focuses on this beneficent relationship, waiting for the least or the greatest scrap with equal intensity, a love affair far gone. Sighing, he lays his head on her bare, sandaled feet, satiated with adoration.

She speaks of her heyday on Madison Avenue: jingles for Pepsi Cola and Maxwell House Coffee, corporate jets to Panama for shoots. Her apartment on Fifth Avenue and house in Kent, Connecticut, however, are for sale.

She owes the IRS $200,000, has further debts of $100,000, is out of work.

"I must not forget my lamb's ears," she says.

"Tell me about them," I say finally. "Why are they so special?"

"I grow butterflies in them. They are full of feeding caterpillars. This big cluster will be totally consumed in a few days," she answers.

"But how do you manage in New York? Where will you track down sufficient lamb's ears?" I ask.

"I go to the flower district, to the farmer's markets. I find enough," she says.

"Why do you do this?" I ask.

"I love butterflies. I love making them. I watch the caterpillars eat the leaves with their powerful jaws. I get up in the night and listen to them munch. I have to see them go into their pupae, into their chrysalides, these metamorphic, diurnal insects, before they take the shape of their imago, their final, winged state."

Bracey, sleeping on her naked feet, stirs, furry images passing through his head, causing him to twitch and snuffle.

In my hallway, do eyeless, furry, ferocious-looking caterpillars crawl over my garden hat and shirt, slither across the old pine captain's chest, hang from the slatted bench, a soft, circus frenzy of mayhem?

"I bring a cloud of butterflies with me to New York," she says. "They fly around my apartment, between my Biedermeier desk and dining table and chairs, among my Dutch still-life paintings of pears and cherries and pitchers of cream. Nymphalis antiopa, Cynthia virginiensis, Polygonia interrogationis, I adore them! I let them out on my fire escape to fly into the New York noontime sky, up the steeple of the Chrysler Building, the radio/TV tower of the Empire State, the square tops of the World Trade Center.

"One morning, when I was taking the elevator to work, a man beside me in the crowded space, said, 'I see a butterfly in your hair!'

"I didn't move, but continued facing forward, staring at the door.

" 'I see another butterfly. My god, your hair is full of butterflies!' he cried.

"The door opened and I walked into the shiny black lacquer lobby of my advertising company lit by recessed lamps in the tall ceiling, the butterflies still in my hair, the man left behind, agitated, amazed.

"I liked that," she says, pushing at her sumptuous, abundant brown hair.

When the time comes to leave, she lifts the lamb's ears out of the vase. I look into them and see a dozen caterpillars eating.

"They will soon be quiescent," she says, sheltering the soft, woolly foliage in her arms.

I think of her imago as she walks toward her car with the bouquet, picture her at the corner of Madison Avenue and Fifty-fifth Street, stopping traffic with butterflies floating about her angel's hair, the dusky purple, sunset red, and iridescent lavender shades of the membranous wings lighting up this corner of the city, this New Yorker with the heart of a naturalist, Amazon explorer in search of insects, adventuress in the jungles of Africa, festooned by canvas bags and butterfly catchers, wearing the order of the Madison Avenue Lepidoptera.

Bracey follows a lost, odoriferous larva as it inches along on five pairs of abdominal prolegs over the hooked tufts of the hall rug, his long, sophisticated nose pressed to the carpet, less than a centimeter behind.

Top of the Stairs

Brenda Gilchrist

"He has difficulty walking and can't stand for long. His back right leg is almost useless. I'm not sure how much longer he can manage to climb the stairs," I say to Dick.

"Just like me!" he cries. "That sounds like me!"

"He can't hear me when I call from behind, unless I yell."

"Yes, yes," he says.

"He caught a terrible virus on our trip and was hospitalized for three days. He almost died."

"One can't be careful enough when one travels," Dick sagely sympathizes.

I am talking about Bracey, my thirteen-year-old Welsh corgi. Dick, of course, is talking about himself.

The conversation repeats itself at parties and in various situations. My generation identifies with my aging dog.

Carol, a friend whose dog died last year, wept steadily for days. "Are dogs sent to us to die before we do so that we will learn what death is about?" she asks.

Bracey is cheerful, doesn't know he has severe leg problems, except when he has trouble getting up the stairs, which cause him more difficulty at times than others. He sits at the bottom and whimpers. He knows he has to make a superdog effort.

I urge him on from the top of the stairs, my heart in my stomach. What will I do when he can't mount them? Carry him up the long flight? He weighs thirty-three pounds.

"Bracey, you can do it. Try harder. Please try harder!"

I am desperate, at the top of the stairs. Fearful of his incapacity, mournful to see him age, to lose him.

"We've got to lick this together."

I organize a house party for a few friends. Reinco calls from Brussels. "I've had this virus all summer. Now they think it may be rheumatoid arthritis. My doctor says I mustn't travel."

Blaikie calls from New York. "My other leg just went out. They think it's osteoarthritis. I'm in a lot of pain. I don't think I can make the trip."

There goes my house party, planned for a year, my friends halted on the bottom step.

"How talented you are," I used to dream of people saying to me. "You paint like Rosa Bonheur; play golf like Babe Dedrikson, tennis like Martina Navratilova; the piano like Bella Davidovich; write like Eudora Welty; act like Tallulah Bankhead."

I wanted to hear stuff like that.

Bracey will learn to manage on three legs. I hope. He needs more time. Despite a thin film over his eyes, they are still fresh; he has pleasures and accomplishments to come.

I wish to tend the rose Lavatera, sulphur-yellow Penstemon, lavender-blue Scabiosa, scarlet runner beans, purplescent cabbage—smack, savor, roll the words on my tongue!—in my garden with zenlike concentration.

Arousal

Early one morning I am awakened by two strangers.
They have dared into my bedroom
with my husband sleeping next to me.
He heard nothing as they slipped through a window.

They are silent but insistent.
One smiles at me warmly.
I cannot resist and smile back.
The other tousles my hair.
My whole body shivers as he sighs for me gently,
his breath cool and crisp.
His companion's gaze stays fixed on me.
I am the object of their desire;
it is a rivalry for my attention.
Ah, the sweet cooling breath again.
I tremble with sensations,
hushed excitement.

My husband stirs and rolls over.
He gets up
shuts the east window
pulls down the shade
falls back into bed.
His breathing is regular.
But I am awake.
I draw him to me.

—Nancy Dobbs Greene

The Offering

Yesterday turkey vultures circled above,
Balanced on treetops, gathered on barns.
Against white snow their hunchbacked silhouettes
Looked foreboding; their pink heads,
Grotesque.

Our friend laughed, "They won't bother you.
But they stink!
Once we had them roosting on our roof.
For two days we banged frying pans.
Finally, they flapped off."

Sometime that night our old dog died.
Unexpectedly.
He had seemed so well.

Iron picks and shovels, we reached for in our grief,
Vibrated from the frigid ground's resistance.
Their ring echoed through the winter valley
Ending desperate efforts at a grave.

O, Ancient Eaters of Carrion,
Shunned Scavengers,
Few defend you. Today I appeal to you
(Not from choice ... not too willingly).
With ice and frozen earth
We had to lay our dear friend out upon your altar.
Do your work.
Free him to roam again.
Leave him clean bones.

—Nancy Dobbs Greene

Alex

Gayle Ashburn Hadley

This look into a dystopian future is an excerpt from Eternal Vigilance, *a novel in progress. Alex, a member of the Worker class, lives in a rigid society that evolved after massive wars decimated most of the population. This world is controlled by a ruling class, the Governors.*

I was afraid – genuinely afraid. Damn that old man! Why did he have to go and remind me about the book? I had nearly managed to forget all about it since Ming Toy gave it to me. Some gift! More like a time bomb ticking away on my bookshelf. Anyone caught reading an unauthorized book could be put in a detention facility for retraining. I had seen some of the people who came out afterwards. They had a vacant look about them, as if they weren't fully there anymore.

I sat on my couch, staring at the bookshelf across the room. Finally, I walked over to it, and looked more closely at my small collection:

"Notification Team Workers' Manual"

"Street Maps of the Old City"

"Supreme Governor Goodwin Harcourt: A Biography"

"Freedom from Family Ties: A Better Way to Live"

"Rules for Good Citizenship"

Except, of course, inside this last book jacket was the book from Ming Toy, just where I had hidden it days before.

I glanced at the window as if someone could be out in the airshaft, spying on me. Then I grabbed the book and sank back onto the couch. As afraid as I was, I was curious too.

I opened the first page. This book seemed to be the collected writings of a Thomas Paine. It was unbelievably ancient, printed in 1776, and then reprinted centuries later in 1995. This must be some kind of history book. I leafed through the brittle pages, coming to a part called "Common Sense."

"Male and female are the distinctions of nature, good and bad the distinctions of heaven; but how a race of men came into the world so exalted above the rest, and distinguished like some new species, is worth inquiring into, and whether they are the means of happiness or of misery to mankind."

I wondered who or what is heaven? Trying to decipher the meaning of this, I found myself wondering how the Governors came to be; why were they smarter than a Worker like me; why did we have to do as they said?

I read on, coming to this:

"Men who look upon themselves born to reign, and others to obey, soon grow insolent; selected from the rest of mankind their minds are early poisoned by importance; and the world they act in differs so materially from the world at large that they have but little opportunity of knowing its true interests, and when they succeed to the government are frequently the most ignorant and unfit of any throughout the dominions."

I didn't think the Governors could be ignorant. They couldn't run everything if they were dumb, either. You must have to be pretty smart to run things. I read that part over and over. Maybe it meant something different, not just dumb: ignorant of real life, my life. How could the Governors, shut up in those buildings with spires, living in private compounds, know about my life? Or that of my partner, Jerry? Or the lives of any of us?

I flipped back to the first part of the book, came across this:

"There never did, there never will, and there never can exist a parliament, or any description of men, or any generation of men, in any country, possessed of the right or the power of binding and controlling posterity to the 'end of time,' or of commanding forever how the world shall be governed, or who shall govern it. Every age and generation must be free to act for itself, in all cases, as the ages and generations which proceeded it."

Well, that did it. I knew what I was reading now. This was subversive. This was not allowed. I don't know what happened to that Paine guy, but I bet they took care of him. And they would take care of me, too. If Ming Toy was mixed up in this sort of thing, it was no wonder she was in big trouble.

My life wasn't exciting; there were things I couldn't do - and I had to do things that I was finding I didn't want to do. At least, not anymore, not lately. I seem to think about what I do more and more and like what I do less and less. Still, it's my life. A safe life.

Without really thinking about it, I jumped up, tore that book into shreds, stuffed it back in the green bag it came in.

* * * *

I went to bed scared and woke up angry. What right had Ming Toy and the old man, Wong, to make trouble for me? I had tried to help somebody out of trouble; they were trying to drag me into it.

After work I found myself storming into the seedy grocery I now thought of as "old Wong's lair," carrying the green bag. Sure enough, there he was, sitting on his stool in the corner behind the counter. I don't know what came over me; the sight of him infuriated me. I vaulted over the counter and threw the bag in his face. I remember I was yelling.

"Hello, Alex," Wong said. He said it just as if nothing were going on. I felt pretty sheepish, but still mad.

"I just want to tell you that you people had no right to palm that book off on me. You have no right to try and get me into trouble too!"

"If you don't like the book, Alex, you don't have to read it. Just give it back to me. Where is it?"

"It's in that bag, Wong. It's torn up, shredded. No evidence. See?"

Suddenly Wong seemed much bigger and taller. He was right in my face.

"You destroyed that book?" His tone was absolutely deadly. I actually flinched, moved back a few steps.

"So what? It was mine. It was a gift, remember?"

His voice seemed to swell. "We don't destroy books, Alex."

Then his tone changed to one of great sadness. His voice even made me feel regretful, too. "Not real books: books of truth, books of history, books of destiny."

Suddenly his arm was around my shoulders. He still seemed to have grown in stature.

"Alex, we need to calm down and talk a bit. Come with me."

"Be very careful," ran through my head. Why I went, I don't know.

He drew back some heavy musty drapes hanging behind the counter and led me into a short narrow corridor. The ceiling was high, the light source a bulb dangling on a black cord. It swayed gently, throwing our shadows on the damp flaking green walls. He pulled the drapes closed behind us. Walking a few steps further he opened a door on the left and beckoned me in with a nod of his head.

The room was small, almost a prisoner's cell. There was a narrow cot, neatly made up, a table and two chairs. Against one wall stood a tall bureau adorned by an ancient hot plate and some kitchen stuff. There was a small sink in one corner. An easy chair and a floor lamp beside it completed the furnishings. The tiny room was scrupulously clean.

Wong said, "We shall have some tea and you shall have an explanation — a history lesson — and some truth, Alex, some truth." He filled a teakettle at the sink and put it on the hot plate.

"The first thing you have to realize, Alex, is that humankind are animals. We have the same basic needs as other animals: to assuage our hunger, to protect ourselves from the elements and to reproduce. What sets us apart from the rest is that we are smarter, we can reason, and more important, we have a moral sense. This loss of innocence, this ability to know right from wrong is what theologians would have us believe is what makes us accursed."

"What's a theologian?"

"We won't go into that now, there aren't many around here these days and it would take too long to explain."

"How are we cursed? What do you mean?"

"We are cursed with a dual nature, the ability to do good and the ability to do evil. The other animals do what their instinct tells them they must do to survive. Mankind goes beyond this. We can empathize with our own kind and engage in acts of kindness, even love, beyond those that are needed to ensure our survival. We can also willfully do great harm and rationalize it or in some cases, even enjoy it.

"The other thing about us is our acquisitiveness. People are greedy. The other animals take what they need; we never seem to have enough. This has led people to seek riches and power, even if they have to enslave fellow humans to attain them. For most of the history of our species we have been making slaves of our own kind in this quest for power and money. Our maker meant us to be free, Alex, not slaves."

"The Governors made us to be free?"

"I don't mean the Governors. I'm talking about the maker, the creator of us all — the one who made the mountains and the seas — the creator of all that is."

I got out of my chair and went over to where Wong sat in his easy chair.

"Well, who is that then?" I asked.

"There is a lot of debate about that, Alex, but the point is, humankind is meant to be free, not enslaved — and you, Alex, are an example of the most complete sort of enslavement ever conceived in the entire history of the human species. You are not held slave by the whip and the lash but by your own mindset.

"You know, I never thought about this in this way before but the current situation is just like the house nigger writ large. You, as a member of the Notification Squad, with your fancy blue tunic, have special privileges over your peers in the Worker class and the Workers have privileges that the Helper class does not have."

"Wong, what are you talking about? What?!"

"I'm sorry, Alex, of course you couldn't know. Let me explain. Years and years ago, toward the very beginning of this country, in the South we had an agrarian economy: large farms called plantations. The owners needed many workers. A brisk and profitable trade sprang up to fill this need. Owners of large ships sailed to Africa and filled their ships with people captured there. They were brought here as slaves to work the plantations. Life as a field slave was gruesome. Some slaves were brought to serve in the slave owners' homes and trained as house servants. Sometimes they were treated almost as part of the family. In some cases they were part of the family though not acknowledged as such. Naturally the field hands resented this more privileged position. The house slaves were called "Uncle Toms" and more crudely, "house niggers." Your more privileged position on the Notification Squad with respect to that of the Helpers, is of the same character."

I started walking around the room, swinging my arms, "I don't feel like a slave. I go about freely. I don't know what you're talking about."

"Exactly my point, Alex. You are so completely enslaved you don't even know it."

This last made me angry. "Now wait just a minute here, Wong. You are going too far!"

"Am I? Who made you? Who is your mother, your father?"

All I could say was, "Well, the Governors created us in the birth nurseries."

"Exactly — in a laboratory. This is not how free men are born. Why did they create you?"

"To serve the state."

His voice became harsh. "The Governors are the state, Alex. You were created to serve other people as a servant, a slave, a robot. Can you wander off, go where you want, do what you want, leave your job, leave this country, wander the world? Can you, Alex, can you?"

"Well, no, but it's dangerous out there. The Governors protect us."

"Bah, Alex, they enslave; they don't protect. Don't take my word for this. You will need to go home and ponder these things. These are new ideas for you."

"I've never heard anyone say things like this, Wong. You must be careful. Someone might hear you. You could be in danger."

"I'm in the danger business, Alex, in case you haven't noticed.

"Now I'm going to tell you something about our country. It's a story of the struggle for man to remain free, and the hardest thing of all, to allow for and protect the freedom of others."

Wong took me back hundreds of years to the time when Europeans first came to this land. He spoke as if to a child but was not talking down to me; not patronizing me. It was as if he knew the reality he described would seem like fantasy to me and he wanted to keep it simple: not just so I would understand, but so I could accept it.

He said that they had lived in a country called England and had crossed the Atlantic Ocean to find a place to practice religious freedom. Then he had to explain religious freedom. Eventually the Europeans, in turn, slaughtered and enslaved the native people who had lived here first.

At this point Wong got up and strode around the room. I could tell he was thinking hard. He picked up a straight chair, placed it in front of his easy chair. He sat down, indicated I should sit opposite. He leaned forward and placed a hand on my arm, looked at me earnestly and said, "This country really began in rebellion against Governors sent from England. There was a revolution in which farmers and shopkeepers fought a trained army. Freedom and independence won, Alex. If we did it once, we can do it again."

"I can't fight them, Wong."

"You don't yet know what you are capable of, Alex."

Wong left nothing out: all the bad things those people have done, all the good, the sacrifices they made for freedom and the many wars that were fought just for freedom. It went on that way right up until now. For a long time it seemed that most people were seeking the good, though many committed terrible acts. Recently, though, the bad guys had won and were now in control.

I don't know what came over me; but when Wong finally stopped talking, I found my cheeks were wet. Me, a grown man, crying. I felt like a fool.

I don't know whether it was the cups of tea, odd tasting but deeply soothing, which Wong kept giving me or the sound of his voice, which rose and fell, swooped, swelled with power and whispered in awe, but I was in that room a very long time. Maybe he was a hypnotist. The story he told was utterly fantastic; he swore that it was the absolute truth; and I wanted to believe him. Oh yes, I wanted to believe that story.

At the last he patted me on the back, saying, "Alex, you are not a political man. The intrigues of resistance are not your forte. But what a grand freedom fighter you could become! Not just yet, however. The time is not right and you are not prepared."

He held out to me another of his dark green cloth bags, like the one the book came in.

"Yes, Alex, another book for you. You will like this one, however. Wait and see. When you have finished it, you will be back for another. Take good care of it. I will see you soon."

He guided me by the arm and I soon found myself out on the sidewalk. The last thing I heard was Wong locking the door behind me. A "CLOSED" sign swung gently on the inside of the glass panel in the door. I discovered that I had been with Wong all night. It was that predawn time when the horizon begins to lighten and a few stars are still visible. I didn't feel a bit tired; I felt exhilarated.

I peeked into the bag I was clutching. I couldn't see the book. It was covered by little paper packages tied with colored string. The labels were in English and Chinese characters: packets of tea, apparently.

A new day was dawning just for me. A really new day. I felt smart, and I smiled as I hugged to myself a very special bit of new knowledge.

Autumn Reflections

Barbara Hattemer

My family's romance with Deer Isle began in the summer of 1931 when my parents camped in tents on a point of land on the southern shore of the island. They lived intimately with the land by day and were lulled to sleep at night listening to waves pounding against granite rocks. Captivated by the shore of Penobscot Bay, they purchased a barren acre to call their own. The lot circled a tidal cove that was empty half of each day. Recently timbered and 300 feet from the water at low tide, it was considered worthless by island natives. My father bought it for $100!

The next summer, I rode the ferry to Deer Isle in my parents' arms. Three months old, I slept in one tent and they in another. Young and adventurous, my parents set about constructing a cabin on their land. Mother pounded away at the pine boards, working side by side with my father. Together, they collected stones from the brook that ran beside the building site and cemented them together to build the great stone fireplace that dominated the living room. Dad crafted well-made cabinets and bookshelves on either side of it. The cabin became one large room with a tiny bedroom, a kitchen, and a porch.

A small dirt lane led away from the main island road into our secluded site. One day, Mom and Dad sat on top of the half-built cabin hammering asphalt shingles into the roof. Suddenly a strange face appeared at the top of the ladder, smiled, and greeted them cheerfully, "Hello, I'm your Fuller Brush man. Can I interest you in any brushes or brooms today?"

I was never sure which story Mother liked best, the Fuller Brush man tracking her in the wilderness or the windstorm that blew my tent down in the middle of the night. In the morning she found me sleeping soundly with the tent draped over the top of my crib, its tall sides keeping me from smothering. The near loss made my parents work doubly hard to finish the cabin. By the end of the summer, proud of their craftsmanship and overjoyed that their dream had become a reality, they moved into their home on the Maine shore.

A few years later, Dad bought the point where they had originally camped. Tiny spruce and fir trees now dotted the land. Shallow soil made from decomposing needles covered dramatic granite ledges that formed a high wall between our land and our neighbor's, then sloped gently toward the bay. This acre had a permanent view of the water and culminated in an extended granite point at low tide. Surrounded by two sand beaches and several tidal pools, it was a child's paradise. About 100 feet from the high tide mark, a great rock left behind by a receding glacier towered several feet above my father's head. I stood at its base and longed to climb to its top.

Eventually my father bought the property between these two lots giving us three acres of continuous shorefront. With it, he acquired what had once been a one-room general store on the island of Vinalhaven. Paneled in old-fashioned, two-inch beadboard with many of the original blown glass windows intact, it had been floated across the bay when it was 100 years old and planted on our shore. My parents added another room and used it as a guesthouse.

For 71 years, I visited Deer Isle every summer, missing only the war years when gas rationing prohibited us from making the trip. When I was a child, the drive from our winter home in Pittsburgh required a whole week. Once we entered the state of Maine, the roads dipped and swerved, repeatedly forcing me to ask my father to pull off the road.

When I was seven years old, I journeyed on the ferry from Sargentville to Deer Isle for the last time. After waiting in line for nearly half a day, it was our turn to drive onto the scow, a large flat boat which held three to five cars at a time. When the cars were loaded, a lobster boat, tied with a long rope that slid back and forth underneath the scow, positioned itself in front and pulled the ferry across Eggemoggin Reach.

I ran to the bow and faced into the wind. A Maine drizzle pelting my cheeks, I imagined I was embarking on a great adventure at sea. As we approached land, I watched the lobster boat turn aside and the attendant take out a large oar, which he used like a rudder to steer the scow as it floated to shore. Quickly he let the raft down on the forward part of the scow and drove pointed bars into the sand on either side to hold the ferry in place while my father and the other drivers drove onto the island.

By 1939, the high bridge over Eggemoggin Reach was completed. As we drove with ease over its length, we struggled to see the magnificent view hidden by the high sides of the bridge. Although it eliminated half a day from the long trip and gave us easy access to the mainland, I treasure the memories of the more romantic voyage on the ferry.

The summer our well ran dry, I was eight years old. What seemed like a tragedy became another adventure. Proud to be able to make such an important contribution, I carried buckets of water from our neighbor's well and placed them on wooden shelves by the kitchen sink. Mother ladled the water from the bucket to a pot and heated it on a green stove fueled by kerosene. Rationing our water use, she took our laundry to the creek and pounded our clothes on the rocks to make them clean.

Once a week, she forced me to bathe in the bay in temperatures ranging from 55° to 59°. Protesting with loud squeals, I developed an enduring love for swimming in icy waters. Perfecting the art of sliding slowly into the water one inch at a time, I emerged refreshed and exhilarated. Tingling sensations on my skin lasted for hours and kept me close to the crackling fire.

Our great room was a large square in which we lived, ate, played games, and assembled jigsaw puzzles. The unfinished cabin walls were covered with brightly colored lobster buoys and unusual pieces of driftwood collected over the years on bay islands. Occasionally Mother allowed us to cook hotdogs on a stick over the open fire in the fireplace. When the logs turned to glowing coals, we roasted marshmallows and made s'mores.

Throughout my childhood, I heard the pulsating bang of our outhouse door as people entered and left it. We used flashlights to find it at night. Inside the cabin, hurricane lamps and candles gave us just enough light to play games after dark. Our rustic lifestyle suited me well and I had no desire for the conveniences that eventually came.

Our summer vacations on the island gave me special time with my parents. Most of the winter they traveled, but in Maine, Mother played endless games with me and spent rainy days helping me master complicated jigsaw puzzles. Dad held school on the beach drawing math problems and diagramming sentences in the sand, giving me an advantage over my classmates. He shared his vast knowledge of land and shore birds, opening my eyes to the wonders of nature.

It was our daily task to carry garbage in pails from the house to the shore and cast it into the ocean on the outgoing tide. We watched seagulls swarm upon it, devouring everything but orange peels, which floated upright out to sea like a parade of toy boats. Dumping garbage in the bay is forbidden now for environmental reasons, but those excursions to the shore to feed the gulls gave my father and me moments of shared intimacy I will never forget.

On picnic days, my father rowed Mom and me and whoever was staying with us at the time to a nearby island and built a fire. Then he rowed back and picked up waiting guests. Mother fried a pound of bacon in an iron skillet and cooked onions and home fries in the bacon grease. As I savored the mingling aromas, I collected firewood to keep the fire going. When Dad returned with visitors, he threw a hand line into the water. Within minutes he caught enough flounder to feed us all. We took their abundance for granted, but now it is rare to catch flounder in the bay.

A brook beside our cabin was a special place where I spent endless hours sailing a small boat and jumping from rock to rock. After a good rain, the water tumbled out of the woods, but in times of drought, the brook was lazy and still. Through open windows in our kitchen we could hear it gurgle cheerfully over the rocks. Even as an adult, cooking never seemed a chore, because I could listen to the brook sing and smell the nearby forest.

The brook mingled with salt water as it flowed through the middle of the cove. At low tide I chased crabs and caught small crayfish. I watched hermit crabs scuttle around in second-hand shells and collected brightly colored periwinkles, limpets, and clamshells bleached white in the summer sun.

We dug clams at low tide in our own front yard. I spotted the holes and my father threw the clam fork behind them, pulling up a mixture of gritty sand and black mud. He spread it on the beach where I combed though it, gathering squirting clams and digging deeper into the holes with my hands. Tugging on the big ones, I never minded the cuts from the sharp shells. Dad hauled the full roller of clams to the edge of the water where I swished it back and forth, washing the clams clean. We covered them with seaweed and set them in the shade outside the cabin door until mealtime.

We had no refrigeration in those days except a single block of ice that was delivered twice a week and stored in a wooden box covered by a heavy tarpaulin. The kitchen and living room floors both contained trap doors. Mother pulled them open and stepped onto a platform, squatting down to store perishable food on small wooden shelves underneath the cabin where it was always cool.

My parents' bedroom held a wall-to-wall double bed with just enough space to pull out the drawers of a built-in bureau on the fourth wall. I slept outside on the sleeping porch. When I awoke, my hair dripped with morning dew but I lay snug in my cot under a pile of blankets, smelling the spruce woods and listening to crows cawing and waves lapping against the granite shore.

At fourteen, I returned after a six-year absence during the war years. *Would it be the delightful shore I remembered or had it been exaggerated in my imagination during the years I longed to be there?* When our car climbed up Caterpillar Hill and I caught sight of Penobscot Bay sparkling in the sunlight, it was even more beautiful than I remembered. The water of the bay reflected the bright blue of the sky, and the green, spruce-covered islands told me I was home.

When we reached our cabin, I ran to our point and collected handfuls of starfish to fill our tidal pool. As I climbed up the granite and dashed toward the pool, I found the 14-year-old boy who lived in the next cabin sketching on the rocks. As very young children, we had played together on the sand beach our parents shared jointly, but this was like meeting him for the first time. He had a crew cut and an impish grin that was both attractive and unsettling.

"Poor little starfish," he said.

I looked at the starfish in my hands. They were wilting into each other from the hot sun and looked like spoonfuls of brightly colored jellies. "We take good care of them in our pool," I protested.

"The gulls will get them in the end. You're not doing them any favor."

It was the first of many spats that helped us become reacquainted. Soon we became inseparable.

Early every morning that summer I'd hear him whistling from the woods, alerting me that he was near. Having slept in long pants and a flannel shirt, I was ready to join him before the rest of the family stirred. He helped me remove the screen panel from the porch as I jumped down to freedom. What wonderful adventures we had every day climbing the shore rocks and gathering starfish. He became my accomplice in replenishing the starfish pool. We rowed across the bay and hiked the islands, picking wild raspberries and gathering baskets of blueberries for our mothers. We imagined our own split-level house on the moss-covered granite ledges between our properties.

At night, we sat side-by-side shining flashlights on the tidal pool. Starfish crawled out from under rocks and moved freely about the pool like slow motion dancers. Sea anemones opened and swayed with the movement of the tide. Crabs scuttled back and forth and crayfish darted about.

We sat for hours on top of the glacial rock I had longed to climb as a child and planned our lives together, but after several years we grew apart and went our separate ways, as often happens with a first love.

When I did marry, my husband and I honeymooned at our cabin on Deer Isle. Fortunately for me, he has always shared my love for the island, and together we had the pleasure of introducing it to our four children. I remember my oldest daughter sitting in the empty cove scooping up handfuls of salty sand, eating it like candy; my first-born son, as a toddler, waddling happily behind us, falling into clefts in the rocks without a whimper.

During his teen years, our second son worked in the bait shop of a lobster dealer. He came home smelling of rotting fish, but elated from camaraderie with local lobstermen. Our youngest daughter discovered a latent interest in the outdoors. She learned to sea kayak on the bay and windsurf on a lake. She climbed mountains in Baxter State Park, and rode her bicycle around Isle au Haut.

Our summers on Deer Isle helped mold us into the people we became. The rocks, the woods, and the sea counterbalanced the influence of city life and town malls. They instilled in us an appreciation for nature that added depth to our life experiences and gave us a love of fundamentals, simplicity and uncontrived beauty.

As we began to extend our stays into the fall, we experienced cold September winds that whistled through bullet holes made by hunters long ago. We stuffed insulation under the floorboards, but squirrels pulled it out and hauled it to their nests. Not wanting to spoil the old cabin's rustic look, we left it as it had always been and built a new house on our remaining lot. On top of the hill that overlooked the point, a November ice storm had felled over sixty trees, all of which had matured during my lifetime. No longer permitted to build on the shore, we took advantage of the cleared site. Seeing the 180° sweep of the bay through the trees was just as lovely as the open view from the old cabin.

* * * *

As I sit looking through the tall picture windows of my new house, I watch leaves fall from brightly painted maples interspersed among the spruces. Like falling stars cascading downward, the leaves garnish the green world of the forest in radiant reds and yellows. My mind photographs the scene, vibrant with life and energy in the crisp October sun.

Nearby, half eaten and curled by inchworms, drab brown leaves hang list-lessly on birch trees. Gusts of wind tear at the tiny threads that hold them to the branches until these leaves, too, fall to the ground.

Now in the autumn of my life, I wonder which leaves represent the legacy I will leave behind. Will my children, my friends, the acquaintances I have touched, remember me like those brilliant leaves that light up the forest? Have I brightened their world, depositing memories they can revisit when they need comfort and love? Or have I impacted them so little, I will be as quickly forgot-ten as those withered leaves that drift beneath the birches?

Falling leaves signal the end of another summer, time to leave the island. I box and store away treasures joyously collected at local craft shows. I cover couches, chairs, and teakwood tables.

The harsh Maine winter will soon arrive replacing leaves with falling snow. Four years ago, an unexpected October storm dropped huge white snowflakes onto our point. They plunged relentlessly downward, unstoppable until they landed gently on my wooden deck and disappeared. Those beautiful white shapes descending silently, elegantly, filled me with warmth in spite of the cold.

Old age is coming as relentlessly as those descending snowflakes. I know the day will come when I can no longer navigate the root-bound paths and rocky shores, but I am grateful for a lifetime of treasured memories on this island. Summers here have brightened all my years and given me deep reser-voirs of joy from which to draw. Like those silent snowflakes, may I find the grace to bear the pains of old age without complaint, and continue to warm those I love with a smile, a hug or a word of comfort.

One thing I know. There is nothing finer my parents could have given me than our vacations here. And I now have the privilege of passing these three acres on to my children to enjoy with their children and grandchildren. With this legacy I am satisfied.

Narcissus at the Window

Turn now
Desert your work
Face the window
Look
See for once the anbient world
Late summer Maine and our cove at high tide
Viewed through a scrim of fog
Or is it sunny there behind your shoulder
Blue sheen against the further shore
Our cove in progress narrowing
Toward emptiness and muck

So indeed the image framed
Now let your eyes deplore
Irregularities untamed
That outward sloping limb of birch
That hanging comb of dead spruce branch
Destroying symmetry
Quickening the urge to prune
What still exceeds the reach
Defies the need for pattern
Obscuring the curve of the shore
The blue echo of a cloudless sky
The arc of osprey's glide
Whose flash of fish retrieved
Puts pattern in a sudden act

Still there is the passing joy
Of patterns formed and dissipated
Replaced by patterns
Nowhere perfectly arranged
Systems gratuitously formed
Clusters of ill-kempt trees shadowing the view
Abandoned for or displaced by savored
Irregularities in the granite of that wall

Through accidents accepting
Disorder gyrates the eye's address
Repudiates the need for rule
Nothing here is stabilized
But instability and desire

Why insist
There is rebellion even in the heart
Where memory mingles delight and fancy
In the frenzy of placidity
As much a product of your sighting
Constant only in mutability

Even in the stricter orders
Shades of chaos adamant
Imply some failed sublimity

Whenever
I look out
I look in

—David Hayman

Scuttling Still

Scuttling
In the far corner
Of my study floor
Dark against polished maple
Dürer's velvet vision
Burns' Wee sleekit creature
Behind the basket
Where it cowered
Frozen
A tiny furry
Mouthful

Exposed
It scuttled
Tentative
To the corner
And again beyond the woven surface
Too pretty
Too vulnerable
By far

No violence in mind
With thoughts of Flaubert
Of Julian's red stain on chapel stone
With miniature reflections
I took Lafcadio's Japanese
And bashed the beast
Not once
It dodged and froze
But twice

Not hard

And then twixt thumb and forefinger
Gently
In memory of Alice
I silently told
That tiny tale
Twitching still
That weightless ball

The distance cross my study
To the sliding Anderson
From which
When opened
It traced
A short trajectory

I gazed with
Certain gladness
At the fresh
Absence of field mouse
In the stain of sunlight
On the gravel

Relief

Only later
An afterthought
I thought to see
How well the grays of mouse
Become the greys of gravel

—*David Hayman*

Where I Find Green in Winter

It is easy in the red shock
of October mountain ash berries
to forget the wasted gray of winter coming,
easy to gasp at swaths of aspen quaking yellow,
easy until only their bleached bones
are left to warm us.

When plants give their cells over
to a final gush of brown,
when wet flakes of white
coat the last bristle of evergreen,
I turn to colors held in the dark hush of forests:

pin-cushion carpets of green fire
flared up from snow-wet soil;
stones humped under glistening skins of moss
laced with the sleek shine of Christmas ferns;
the cream-green underbelly of sphagnum
heaved up through a frozen night.

—Crystal Neoma Hitchings

Regeneration: a history of landscape
for my father

1.
In the cedar swamp, no cedar grows.
Fir pokes shy from sphagnum moss, pine scrambles,
water moves southwest, toward sun.

You talk about runaway dogs, deer chasing,
an offered-up carcass on a pile of fresh cedar posts,
the old man's saw buzzing for days.

I cannot say "Now there is nothing."
There is you. There is me. There is crow flying.
Cedar seeds wait in the earth.

2.
Near the rock-crack-cave,
porcupine pulls oak into its belly, strip by strip,
lips move over stained teeth;
bone-bare branches jut startled
toward winter chill, already dying.

You hesitate to step over the crack's deep maw;
in its gut, smoothed by the slow wipe of time,
the girl who once trembled to think what creatures dwelled here —
now I seek their sweet musk.

3.
Boundaries stretch into distance like veins —
dark ropes of spruce run up ridges of granite,
the tall one marking a turn;
white fields where ghosts of fire burn,
pocked with young oak, sliced
by birch-clogged arteries of road.

Earth pulses with blood of birthing.
Pins in ledge say here and here.
Names fall from your mouth,
who owned what when;
maps unfold in your eyes,
your compass points to me.

—Crystal Neoma Hitchings

The Place of Forgetting

on contemplating my thirtieth birthday

In the mirror, she can't find herself.

Tidy arrangements of doodads and dreams
mark her passing: pussy willows dry in jars;
photos smile from the refrigerator.
She sips tea that doesn't warm her
with lips that long to taste fire.

Far beyond walls, something beckons.

She rises, walks past dead flowers, empty photos,
out into dampness, earth-smell,
closes a door behind her.

Bare toes move into forest.

Here, only snuffle of deer,
love song of wind,
mushrooms pushing at earth.
Leaves reach for skin.
Berries whisper to tongue.

She bends, soft ground,
presses knees to chest, becomes small,
creeps between stones,
laps dew from cupped petals;
cloth shreds, unravels,
disappears behind bushes.

Far beyond her, in the place of forgetting,
spiders spin webs over windows,
around chair backs,
beetles feast on boards,
skunks lay babies down in closets,
flowers grow over the roof,

a telephone rings, unanswered.

—*Crystal Neoma Hitchings*

Spotted Salamander and Gardener

He comes up dumb and blind in a shovelful of mud,
translucent eyelids squeezed against a sudden terranean glare,
fat and still, as if dead.

In terror I poke him, and he shifts,
slow as the ooze he comes from.

I have never before seen those blue dots,
electric splashes in dull mud,
that fat slow jelly body
woken from the thickness of sleep,
a quiet miracle.

When I place him down, far from my digging,
he awakens at the touch of wet earth,
slipping fast beneath muddied water.
My palm tingles, alive with the touch of his world.

I move back to where I found him.
My job here is to tear out those sedges hanging
low and messy into the water,
sedges whose dark canopy once held him.

I slice my weapon into the bank,
watching every shovelful
for spotted salamander halves.

—Crystal Neoma Hitchings

Blue Cloud Larkspur

Who knows about the tears
behind the blue of eyes
or the feathering out of sorrow
into constellations of laughter
at the corners of life?
Or the yearning:
the seeds of anon and again
springing up from shallow roots
from stock and stem
from webs of green fragility
into an amazement of stars,
bluestruck suns,
illimitable skies?

—Nancy B. Hodermarsky

Of Luminescence

We go on sea shells,
moonlit,
ankle deep in luminescence,
floating, lambent, disembodied,
a waking of plankton
at ocean s edge;

and drift through fields
knee deep in noontide,
purple vetch, buttercup,
bluet, violet, forget-me-not,
of beyond calling back delight;

so like the stones full of longing
ever pushing up from beneath,
we breathe
in each other, taste salt,
touch, all over,
without hands.

—Nancy B. Hodermarsky

Nigella

Exotica they called me
down at Fishermen's Friend
where ballet-skirted, midsummer,
I stood at the counter
and shimmered mascara into the stews
they were eating, those men,
young and strong,
who longed to brush fingers upon
some chevaux de Venus.

Now on the threshhold of autumn,
nerve ended, I dance barefooted
at the end of the garden,
dance out of my hand-me-down clothes,
exposing a belly too large for the birthing,
whirling, winding, flinging black seeds
of Love-in-a-Mist onto isolate ground,
a spiralling down to die
and survive
in the careless arms of another.

—Nancy B. Hodermarsky

The Journey Home

On that next to last journey
he asked to park on the barrens,
those dying blueberry fields,
bleeding their crazy reds, magentas, alizarins
down into autumn.
I held to the broken cage of his breath,
laid my head on his heart,
his grossly irregular heart,
that muscle, worn sore by fibrillations
and portioned out bit by bit to clots.

But he reaches
with his strong forearm to lift me from
that cavernous atrial chamber.
He whispers his nonsense into my breasts,
one hand cupping mine around life;
the other, slipping down, pleasure riding far from the barrens
all those byways of desire
to a beloved island,
heading home.

—Nancy B. Hodermarsky

House of the Dead

Horns of past moons
Scratch the dust.
Tattered rugs worn thin.
Afraid to turn the key,
I stand halting.
Beyond the threshold
Dissolved in vinegar
My shadow too, could disappear.

—Billie Hotaling

Sisters

Because you study classics
And speak French,
Discussing art criticism,
You think I lack sophistication.
Because I work in ghettos
With small children,
Face runny noses and ragged clothing,
I think you lack humanity.
When we meet on holidays,
Weddings, anniversaries,
We talk of recipes,
House decoration, gardening.

Still, I remember
Two little girls
Reading around the table,
Sledding on the golf course hill,
Playing duets at one piano.

—Billie Hotaling

Reality

My love and I lived on a cliff.
Pinned to the crest
By one small
If.

We didn't live there long, because
In time our If
Turned into
Was.

—Billie Hotaling

Reflections

Familiar songs pressed in wax
Still quicken the listening heart;
Lavender in pages
Holds the scent of spring.
Landscapes on museum walls
Reflect a life
Unchanging.

Until I pass the mirror
It never occurs to me
That I am
Old.

—Billie Hotaling

Wren's Nest Point

Some houses are cozy and small,
Holding you in.

But a new place, with windows
That are taller than one's own view,
Exhilarates a dancing mind.

Outside the blinds
Dark sunlight calls
And trunks of trees stand sentinel.

—D Immonen

Sunshine Road

Exploring,
Day heavy with impending storm,
This Maine has hints of the Orient;
Tibet, colors of prayer flags—
Bright blues, gashes of yellow orange, impossible green.

Here is a three-sided shed
Lined with firewood,
Decorated with silver cobwebs.
And there is smooth birchbark on the ground,
To write letters to friends who are children.

—D Immonen

Assignment

Write about an object.

An object?
What the hell kind of object
am I going to write about
this time of night
when all I want to do
is curl up with a good book,
long enough to put me to sleep.
Object.
I'm looking around the room
to see if there is a likely subject.
My bedroom slippers are objects.
But, what can I say about them
except that they are falling-apart-old
and full of holes.
Not very interesting.
I guess I could write about the alarm clock.
But it's a digital clock
with fiery red numbers
that pop out at me relentlessly.
No.
But I could write about
Bill's tattered, tan sweater
hanging over the rattan chair.
I wear it now
because it's cuddly and warm
and sometimes I pretend
his arms are still in it
when I slip it on.

—Judith Ingram

Don't see old

When you look at her,
don't see old.
And never, never
say elderly.
It's a rotten word,
conjured up
by the same mentality
that first called
this loser time of life
the golden years.
A sign in a store window said …
For the elderly, over 65 …
Standing there, palpitating, eyes alight,
she turned to Dan,
Good Lord, Dan,
would you call me elderly?

She still dances all night at Sam's Place on the boardwalk.
She still skinny dips in the star studded bay.
She still pushes baby carriages
and swishes a little, too.
She still has the cutest fanny,
like he said when she was twenty.
And if a smart, young fella
is nice to her and dimples when he smiles,
She will adopt him and squeeze him
and take him home with her.
Her heart sings and soars and
she still gets little itches.
So when you look at her,
don't see old.

—Judith Ingram

Haircut

Chauffeuring her husband
who's no longer able to drive,
she drops him off
at Leroy's barber shop,
a kitchen converted
for chopping hair
instead of vegetables.
Eight to twelve, every Saturday morning
the old men gather there,
lined up against the wall
in creaky, wooden chairs,
chattering in their island patois,
hashing over the town news.
… enjoyin' theyselves and
not too eagah to be called
up to the chayah,
afeared a missin' somethin' …

Trying to time it just right,
she arrives back at Leroy's
and sees him standing
alongside the country road.
His hair has been cut … no question.
She stops the car
a few feet from him
and leans out the open window.
Laughingly, she calls,
"Hi … are you waiting for a trolley car?"
Looking directly at her,
he answers,
"No, I'm waiting for my wife
to come and pick me up."

—*Judith Ingram*

Don't feed them too many apples

Seven heifers inhabited
our five enclosed acres.
Brown and white,
nuzzling green grasses,
the sun warm on their backs.
Mr. Warren, the farmer
who rented our land,
told the children,
Don't feed them too many apples,
it will make them loose.
Nicola looked at me and asked
What's loose?
When the spring ran dry,
we put an old white porcelain tub
in the field.
The children kept it filled with water.
We have photographs of them
holding the hose, their heads
not much higher
than the rim of the tub.
For several years,
those cows were our entertainment.
But, we were careful not to feed them
too many apples.
And then the time came
when they got through the fence
into Bill's vegetable garden.
What they didn't eat,
they mashed to fodder.
Mr. Warren offered to pay.
But there's no price
for time and hard work and love.
So the cows went back to Mr. Warren's.
Now, the years … and the children have gone, too.
All that remains by the edge of the field
is the old, white porcelain tub.

—*Judith Ingram*

To Alice Who Taught Me About Poems

I remember when we would stay up all night
heading down to the village to watch the baker

make the doughnuts, the greasy O's rising
miraculously in the oil. I'm sure he was wondering

why jerked up college kids would come down the hill to visit him:
He was at work, while we were at discovery. Some jobs

can be discoveries, not like the ones famous scientists make
but like those I made before I visited you that summer.

I was working in the gas station, learning to stop the pump
just right on the dollar, not going over a penny, or cleaning

the windshields perfectly with the squeegee, the water
running down like a light show on the shadow of the dash board.

I hitchhiked from Boston to Maine to visit you at your cottage,
getting a long ride in a hippie's recycled delivery van past the hulks

of the schooners rotting in the harbor in Wiscasset, past
the tacky souvenirs in Perry's Nut House in Befast,

until I was dropped off on route 15, still 40 miles away,
in the mosquito-filled dusk near the humming and flickering

lights of the gas station, like an Edward Hopper painting come to life.
How is it when night comes on we can feel so alive?

The darkness is surrounding us and we're standing
with our hopeful thumbs out waiting for a ride.

—Stuart Kestenbaum

When I First Heard Noah's Story How God Gave a Sign That the Earth Would Never Be Flooded Again I Had Never Seen a Rainbow

So when it rained hard on the New Jersey streets,
when the rain made little domes as it struck the asphalt
and torrents rushed down by the curbs
and into the storm sewer, the rainbows appeared.
The illuminated oil slicks, God's multi-colored promise,
shone on the streets, floating on puddles
glistening on the wet blacktop.
The world was new again and water
was dripping off the leaves of the sheltering maples.
God was in Heaven and I was riding
my bike, fast, through the puddles.
There were no doves with olive branches
but their relatives, the pigeons,
slapped their wings as they left earth
and banked gracefully in unison.
And how far off was I with the rainbows?
Weren't the oil slicks a kind of covenant
that had traveled from the 4.6 billion-year-old-sun
down to the earth, growing prehistoric plants
that rose again as oil and powered and lubricated
the engines of Fords and Buicks?
May I be forgiven for misinterpreting
an old story. It was all I knew
and I was making the best of it.

—*Stuart Kestenbaum*

Trough and Crest

Cordis B. Lichten

Then they cried out to the Lord in their trouble, and he brought them out of their distress.

He stilled the storm to a whisper; the waves of the sea were hushed.

They were glad when it grew calm, and he guided them to their desired haven.

Let them give thanks to the Lord for his unfailing love, and his wonderful deeds for men.

—Psalm 107: 28 – 31   Holy Bible, New International Version.

Dawn was barely perceptible seven miles east of Little Cod Rock. The marine forecast called for seas 3-5 feet but Danny thought these swells were more like 5-8. Winds had to be gusting to at least 50 knots. Leaden sea and leaden sky ran together, confused, as the Li'l Missie toughed along straining against uneven seas and wind.

The NOAA radio forecast at 6 AM predicted foul weather. The first tropical system of the season was moving in from the Southwest later this afternoon. Last week the fog had stymied the Bar Harbor whale watch fleet and kept the vacationers in town instead. Along the coast from Hatteras to Halifax today, forward-thinking fishermen were testing their spotlights so they could check their boats from shore tonight. Danny was intent on baiting up all his lobster pots before the high seas and bad conditions hit.

With the seas kicking up, items and equipment on the Li'l Missie that usually were secure could work loose. Danny scraped his graying forelock with the back of his hand, tipped his Red Sox cap back on, and ran through a mental list of what could go wrong out here. The brackets holding the battery in place could give way. He'd been meaning to replace them. Move battery brackets to number one position on the to-do list. He thought about shipworms moving up the coast and how quickly they could drill a hull, turn it into sponge. Better paint the bottom this year, too.

Sweat ran down Danny's sides under his T-shirt and his lips were dry. He was driving the boat, as hard as he dared, to his secret, productive hole off Hebron Ledge. He patted his back pocket absently – yes, wallet still there, with two Red Sox tickets for the August 15 game against the Yanks. He took another sip of cold, bitter coffee from the Red Sox cup that fit in the holder at the helm. He choked, recovered, then drank the last of the coffee to get the grains of undissolved sugar at the bottom.

He peered out around the starboard bow, watching for his buoys in the spume. It was too much trouble to pick up the binoculars that hung by the helm, and too hard to focus in these seas anyway. He knew he had about twenty pots out here at the edge of the shelf. The depth made fishing a borderline activity, but then fishing was borderline anyway. There were some fat lobsters out here at this time in the summer. Maybe these guys had put off going inshore with the bulk of the population, for reasons no one understood. Last year he had caught seven keepers in one trap out here. This might have been the talk of the day at the dock if he had told a soul.

The radio was silent and he wondered if he had lost it altogether when he heard Wyman talking as though through a long tube. "Li'l Missie Li'l Missie this is Wannabe, switch to channel 9?"

He yanked the transmitter out of its hook and spoke into it quickly, "Wannabe, this is Li'l Missie, going to channel 9." Then, over on the empty channel, he said, "I'm out in the back forty picking up my last few before the storm gets here. Come on over and watch the ball game with me later, why don'tcha. Over."

"Yeah, Dan, the forecast was updated. They're sayin' the winds are going to pick up soon. You and me are the only ones out here today. I'm gonna head in. Let me talk some sense into you. Let's go in, over."

"Wyman, don't be an old woman. I'll be done soon and follow you. My radio's going bad again, so if you don't get me, don't worry. Li'l Missie out."

"Suit yerself, Danny. But I don't think it's a good idea. They're sayin' …" but Wyman's voice cut out, then sputtered as indecipherable honks, and then the radio was dead. Daniel spotted one of his buoys off the port bow and soon forgot that Wyman had more to say.

There was some reassurance in the rhythm of hauling pots, sizing the lobsters, tossing back the small ones and those with a V-notched tail, then baiting traps and setting them back overboard. It would have been easier with Tod in the stern, especially in all this wind, but Daniel was used to working alone and usually he enjoyed the exertion.

Today, though, the relentless seas and the falling barometer brought an urgency to the task. Every so often the starboard bow dipped into a wave and the spray dashed back into the house. But Daniel was pleased to see the size of the lobsters in the traps. Yessuh, that's what we came out here for.

The waves continued to build. New curtains of rain spattered along the sea and sheeted across the Plexiglas windows of the cabin. Daniel was wet inside his slicker. He searched for his last six pots. He thought the boat drove especially heavy and was harder to turn than usual. Finally he spied his merry red and orange buoy up ahead, so he throttled the engine back and tried to bring the boat up into the wind. Now he was sure Li'l Missie handled more sluggishly than she should, even in these bad conditions.

The water in the bilge had been held in the stern while the boat made headway through the waves, but decceleration brought its momentum rushing forward into the bow. Daniel could feel the stern rise, and he realized that the water in the bilge must have shifted forward. Now it was even harder to steer. To a casual guest aboard the Li'l Missie most of this would have gone unnoticed in the wind and waves. To Daniel it was as obvious as a neon sign. The bow was down, so he must have a leak.

He lurched below, intending to pull up the cabin sole to check the bilge, but as soon as he stepped through the hatch he could see it was big trouble. An especially large swell knocked him against the hatch door and he held on for a moment, flailing for a handhold. He saw the swirl of black water in the cabin, with paper cups, a life jacket, motor oil jugs, an empty water jug, and cigarette butts in an unappetizing stew. He reached up to flick the switch on the bilge pump but there was no response. Had the battery come loose and knocked against the through-hull for the sonar? That would explain the poor steering capability. The resulting leak might not be detected until he slowed the boat to haul a pot. Such a leak could short out all the electrical circuitry. No automatic bilge pump, no radio, no way to call in a May Day. He fished up the dripping life jacket from the dizzying flood in the cabin sole. He struggled into it with one hand and fumbled with the clasps while gripping the bulkhead with the other.

Daniel liked to think of himself as cool in a crisis. But just now he felt nauseous and wished he had sprung for that survival suit. All at once that $259 didn't seem to be such a high price after all. He looked below again and considered wading through the water to pull out the hand pump that was stashed forward. Just then the boat began to roll in a slow broach. The port wash-rail dipped into the sea and a wall of water came across the deck. The Li'l Missie slowly shook herself free but rode lower still.

Water filled Daniel's knee-high boots. This Gulf of Maine water was too cold for a swimmer to last long, even in late July. He stepped over the helm and regained his balance, then throttled the engine up. He wrestled the helm over with all his strength. He tried to bring the bow again back into the wind, but the Li'l Missie hardly steered at all.

How far am I from Dowitcher Island? He drew lines on the nautical chart in his mind and estimated the distance. Size of swells, storm coming in… God, I'm too far out. There's nothing here but Devil's Idea and that's a godforsaken ledge submerged at high tide. At low tide, it was a boiling cauldron with waves shooting up as they notched into the rock. And Wyman's headed in already.

He toggled the bilge pump over and over, but there was no response. The engine had developed a high whine and was shuddering, with the prop exposed to air intermittently as the seas knocked the boat about – a cat, teasing its living prey. Now and then a larger swell knocked at the hull and dumped cold saltwater over the side into the stern deck. Li'l Missie was going down.

Danny stood at the helm staring out over the bow. The hammering scream of the engine filled his ears. He thought, This has been a pretty good boat. I should have kept up with the maintenance schedule I made out years ago. That was a reasonable schedule, and it would have made a difference, I bet. But then, when it's your time to go, I guess it's just time. Period.

Now the foredeck was awash and the seas were churning all around the Li'l Missie with their tops blowing off and ragged crests descending into valleys of lumpish dark grey. It wasn't the worst Daniel had ever seen, but close to it. He checked his watch – only 8:30 AM and so much has happened already today!

He thought about Gina, how dear she was to him. I shouldn't have run away to play so many times, he thought. I could have stayed home more, helped her with her little projects. Could have redone the bathroom, even the kitchen. She's been a good wife, better than I deserve. Maybe should have rototilled the garden for her, painted the house, brought her some roses, taken her to Cap'n Scott's Restaurant over in Gilbertville more than once a summer.

What would happen to Tod? That boy needs a father, and I haven't been much of an example. Lewis would have kept him in line. Or maybe not, but at least Tod would have had a father. I just let him come along with me but I didn't really show him how to make a clean life. Didn't give him wisdom. Now who will be there for him, besides Max?

Maxine. She was his big sister, the one he turned to when things were going wrong. She would be praying about now, he realized. I could pray, if I knew how. He focused his thoughts and said: God, it's me here. Get me out of this mess. I want to live.

Daniel considered making God a promise in return for letting him live, but thought that lacked sincerety, given that he hadn't been to church in years. When he said the name of Jesus it was usually in an exclamation of exasperation or pain.

I won't lie to you, Lord. I'm not much of a believer out here, but I do want to live. Give me another chance.

Now a wave came up rapidly, larger than the others, and from the starboard quarter – a cross sea. It tilted the Li'l Missie far over and when she rolled back, the sea poured in and filled the aft deck in a matter of seconds. The greatest shock was when his feet were swept out from under him, and he lost contact with the deck. No longer captain of his ship, Daniel released his hold on the helm as he kicked off his boots. He was swimming in the cold bath, away from the boat as fast as he could, awkward in the bulky life jacket. Some fishermen got pulled down with their sinking vessels; he was determined not to let this happen to him.

The sky was an impenetrable gray, and the sea below him extended 93 fathoms to his own lobster traps. This was no place for a swimmer. A wave bore down on him, towering over him and breaking toward him. This is some predicament. I sure got in deep this time, he thought. Miles from nowhere and a storm coming. Nice goin', Moore, he scolded, calling himself by his last name only in extreme circumstances. He soon grew tired of guessing whether the coming wave would wash over his head.

"Come get me, Lord, and get me quick!" called Daniel, but there was no reply that he could hear and he got a mouthful of salt water. He decided he'd just have to talk to the Lord with his mouth closed.

* * * *

There was a church bell ringing. No, a car horn blaring, or no, it must be a primitive alarm that got set off when someone bumped the car even slightly. Kids, goofing around, hit the car as they ran past, just to get the alarm going. The neighborhood must be alerted by now. Couldn't someone figure out how to turn that alarm off? Maybe disconnect it underneath somehow. But it must be a church bell. Daniel was annoyed that the bell sounded at odd intervals. Couldn't the bell ringer keep a rhythm? Get someone else for that task.

A wave slapped him in the face. He spluttered and choked. Gradually he realized that he was alive, floating in the Atlantic Ocean with nothing between him and his Maker but a cheap life jacket. The loss of the Li'l Missie was something he must have imagined; surely it was nearby, waiting for him to climb back aboard. No insurance, damn it all.

The bell was clanging so loud, he could not ignore it. He wanted to put his fingers in his ears. He tried to turn and look around as he rode to the crest of the wave, but he could not make his arms or legs move. Hypothermia was setting in, or perhaps it was already advanced. Daniel tried to remember what to do about hypothermia: wrap the victim in warm blankets; give warm drinks. His thoughts were a blur.

Out of the corner of his eye he caught a glimpse of a bell buoy, steel painted red and white, leaning in the waves amid wind and fog. Was he imagining this? A wave lifted him and he saw it again. It was enormous, and nearby, and hope warmed his synapses. He lost sight of it again as he descended into the trough, but as the energy of the wave boosted him up into the crest, he saw it, and found a little energy to swim toward it. In its low-tech way, the buoy was doing its job faithfully as always. Now it was so close he could almost reach out and touch it, and then a wave knocked it out of reach. Now closer, now farther. Warmer, warmer, hot! No, cooler, cold.

I have to try harder. He realized the gravity of his situation, and summoned his strength. He gauged the speed and height of the waves around him. Life or death, life or death. Now the buoy was near. He reached up with one arm, then the other, and grabbed at a steel rod above the flotation on the buoy. The towering buoy rocked away from him, capricious as a naughty child. It mocked him, clanging loud, and he struggled after it. The effort seemed to get his blood flowing, but again the buoy swept out of reach, ringing clumsily as it went.

Tears of desparation sprang to his eyes, but Daniel concentrated on reaching and grasping the steel rod. He descended into a trough and lost sight of it again.

When the buoy leaned briefly toward him, he grabbed and held with all his might. He was lifted out of the water as the buoy rolled away again. Legs dangling, he held on with anguish and determination. Maybe I can still get to that Sox game after all, he thought, and the anticipation of the trip to Boston in late August gave him new strength.

With difficulty he worked one shaking leg up and over the rod and made his way into the center of the buoy, wedging himself against it. He wrapped an arm around the upright steel and locked his fingers, shivering mightily. He watched the sheets of rain on the waves and thought he must not be far from where he had calculated that the Don had sunk on June 29, 1941. He traced back through his memory for the details of that loss of 34 souls. He realized that he would forever wear the blame for sinking his own boat, just as the memory of the captain of the Don bore infamy long since that tragic event. Other maritime history buffs would read about the Li'l Missie and think what a careless dolt he had been. History will not be kind to me, he realized. But I'm alive.

The wind tore across the steel of the buoy, the jangle of the bell pierced his brain, and the rain drummed his bowed head. He was exultant as though he had been washed ashore on a palm-laden desert island with a pile of ripe coconuts to greet him. But no one knew where he was, and he would not be found before hypothermia finished him off. The buoy leaned and swayed in the seas, and the bell clanged above his head. Too loud. When I feel a little better, I'm going to tie that clapper off with the strap of this life jacket, he decided. Then, with his body tightly worked into the buoy, he sank again into unconsciousness.

* * * *

The lights were always on at Coast Community Hospital. In all the patients' rooms the night lights could not be turned off. It was hard to sleep, at least for Daniel. He was afraid to close his eyes because every time he did, a vertigo of rocking brought a fresh rush of panic. In his mind he was on the buoy again, swaying with the seas, too cold to move. It was better if he did not close his eyes, but he had to blink now and then.

He traced the patterns in the ceiling tiles with his eyes, over and over, and each time, he could see more of the night sky. The Big Dipper. Then Polaris, in direct line from the outer lip of the cup. Then the Little Dipper, with Polaris at the end of its handle. Cassiopeia. The Pleiades. Back to Polaris. Everything turned but Polaris. He could find them all in the tiles above his bed, by the dim blue-green light of the hospital room. Sometimes they turned so fast that he had to rest his eye on the corner of the room, pin his gaze on that corner until the stars stopped turning. He had been doing this for hours.

Gina would come again in the morning. For now, he could find his favorite constellations in the flimsy bit of civilization five feet above his head. He felt as though he had been put through a washing machine, spun almost dry, thrown in the drier, and then hung out on the line for a good airing.

At 1:30 AM the older nurse with the curly hair came to check his vitals. He was staring up at the ceiling. He wanted to ask if his rescue had made the 11 o'clock news. He wanted to connect with her, to make a little joke so that she would smile. But instead he said, "I'm alive." It was a whisper, or a croak. She glanced briefly at his face, placed a cool palm on his forehead, and turned away to continue her rounds.

Wyman was the hero. At his insistence the Coast Guard had come out to find Daniel when the Li'l Missie was still out at noon two days before. Wyman hated hospitals but he was appreciative of the blueberry pie Maxine delivered to his house yesterday.

I'm a rich man, Daniel thought. I'll get back out there sometime to get those big fat lobsters. He closed his eyes and the room reeled. But this time he rode with it, dizzy, and full of praise.

(This is an excerpt from an unpublished novel.)

The Inclined Plane

The image of the face and the real thing
form in adjacent windows, opposite reflecting,
Frosted by a glistening dust. Perhaps
With a pair of scissors
I could disassemble them,
Recompose the genes over long distances
Travelled in a clip,
And over coffee
Bring that face,
Stunned with sudden gravity,
In alignment with its pair
And interrupt their symmetry;
Move the middle closer to the end …
It would require massive reconstruction,
Rewiring circuits
In the template of the hand
To reset the meter a half step
From the metronome,
Set the heart just behind the eye,
Adjust the focus
So that the end would be clear
Only at the beginning.

—*David Lund*

Legacy

The debts I'll finally forgive
    And guilt will draw no further interest.
I've paid my dues,
    Scattering regrets like pennies.
My wealth of sins and lapses,
    Unfortunate omissions,
I leave to charity.
    I'll spare compassion
For another season.

And for my children
    And my friends
Morsels of devotion, stored up love
    In interrupted rhyme,
And quiet faiths, colors of the dawn
    Preserved in moonstone
Set in moss against the frost.

For the world –
    A small harvest of imaginings
From the painter's eye,
    Offerings of pungent fruit
From orchards burst wild and cultivated
    Of phantoms in slow-burning hues
Copper roses saffrons rusts jade blues
    Of interweaving leaves and shoots
From which the heart will leap.

—*David Lund*

The Night Manager

Deborah Wedgwood Marshall

The first time I saw the fat lady, she was peddling her homemade milk-chocolate lollipops; the 45-cent Smurf pop, a 75-cent Goofy with the stick up his ass and Darth Vader for $1.00, just as sinister in chocolate as on the Big Screen. The way she waddled into the Joint with her cheap chocolates, her gaudy tent dress and the scent of drug store perfume trailing after her, impressed me as "tacky." I wondered if Boss and Partner would feel the same as I did about this scene. I thought, probably, then felt a bit ashamed for mean thinking so I decided to be cool, and I hid my smile behind my hand.

As with most girls, I was taught that fat is not beautiful – by every maga-zine, parental conditioning, my peers, you name it. I always felt that when I gained weight I was ugly, even though I never even came close to being as big as this woman was. Boss and Partner were also not without their prejudices. Partner especially, had an aversion to people who were even slightly heavy. Anyway, the day the fat lady entered the Joint, Partner was there and hesitantly accepted the chocolates on consignment, and while she signed her name to the contract, Partner and I exchanged grins and quickly looked away from each other. We would have burst out laughing otherwise.

When she left, I laughed nervously when Partner said, "Arnold Schwarzenegger, watch out!" Her arms were probably the biggest ones I'd ever seen. I felt relieved that I wasn't the only bigot on duty that day.

She left her rack of lollipops on the counter, where they sat for two weeks. Occasionally, one of the employees at the Joint would pick one up on the way by, but the product didn't sell, and Partner had to ask her not to bring anymore.

Often when I see a face, I see it often. In the case of the fat lady, she suddenly seemed to have become a fixture around town. When I was working at the Joint with Partner she would be there feeding pizza to her brood. When I worked at the Spoon with Boss, she would bring them by for ice cream. When it was ice cream, she would always order five baby cones for her five boys and an empty sugar cone for her baby daughter, and she always ordered the largest chocolate cone for herself. I wondered about that big ice cream cone and her size. God, if I was that big, I'd be so embarrassed to be seen eating all that fattening stuff. Did she know that people snickered at how big she was? 400 pounds, maybe? More? I wondered about her self-esteem, what it would feel like to be that big. Really, she could almost have been in a circus. I didn't like being around her. Besides her size, I was just plain uncomfortable around her. She gave me the creeps. But as with most odd things we soon got used to her being around.

I found out her name was Rita Junkins. I found out that she was looking for work, and I found out that Boss was looking to hire.

I had been dating Boss for a few months, as well as working at the Joint with him until the summer season started, which was when Partner showed up to run it. Boss and I then opened up the Spoon and decided to run the place together 'til fall. I'd been so damn lucky to get a good scholarship at the University, but I still had to supplement tuition. I loved that Boss was so supportive and proud of me. He and I could each make a bundle of money this summer. As in most relationships, there were ups and downs, but we were pretty close, and we also each had our independence. We discussed business though he and Partner were the ones in charge of hiring and firing. When he told me one day that he wanted to hire Rita Junkins to work at the Spoon, I was surprised. He'd certainly done his share of laughing and making jokes about her!

"She's too big to move around in the Spoon," I objected. "It's only a small take-out, Boss!" God, I was shocked at this turn of events. I immediately tried to come up with any excuse not to hire the woman. "She's too huge! She's too short! What will she do with her kids?"

I felt creepy vibes around Rita, but with all that, I admired the way she handled her kids. For instance, she didn't yell at them all the time the way I had with mine. All she had to do was give them a certain quick look and they toed the line, pronto. I got the idea they were scared of her.

The day Rita Junkins hired on at the Spoon, I was leery, but my objections fell on Boss's deaf ears.

The day Rita Junkins hired on, Boss said to me, "Rita will be here at 4:00. I made a mistake and double booked a meeting with the bank at 3:30 ... so, will you please, please show her the ropes 'til I get back?" He took me in his arms and gave me a great big hug and a sweet kiss.

"Yes, sir, Boss," I said, sighing.

Although I was somewhat apprehensive, never having trained anyone before, I was also turned on. I wished that Boss would take me downstairs for a few minutes, instead of making me do his dirty work. But the time was well past 3:15 and Boss had to make his exit.

A little more than half an hour later, Rita made her appearance.

"Hiya, Rita. Where are the little boys and girl today? I'm Pats, and Boss asked me to show you how this operation works. Welcome to the Spoon!" I was doing OK with this.

"Uh, Hi Pats. Yeh, the kids is with my neighbor. I'm real glad to be workin' again. I like evenings workin' 'cause that's when the kids is in bed and it's real lonely with the old man away. My folks was here but now they moved too far to visit easy. Hey, this place ain't too bad in here!"

I thought, "Ohmygod" and "I should show her how to do everything wrong ... then, no, better be a good girl!" My bad thoughts were fleeting, and in my organized way, I showed Rita the preparation, the cooking, and the serving of all the food we sold at the Spoon, and answered all her questions. She had worked at fast-food places before so she already knew something about it. She was uneducated and not very classy, but she wasn't dumb. Low class.

I liked having a clean "operating theatre," as I called the kitchen, especially when the customers could look in the windows and easily see what was happening inside. I'm sure they didn't like seeing flies all over the ice cream machine and on the counters and in the sink.

Rita and her kids always looked clean, and she readily agreed with me when I said, "If you have time to lean, you have time to clean!"

We were able to talk a little about raising children. We learned some things about each other. I tried to avoid touching her or looking at her, which was pretty difficult. She was so big! It was uncomfortable for me to be around her. I learned that her husband was her second and that he had just joined the Merchant Marines, shipped out. She expected him home by winter.

"I'm intrigued!" I thought.

Rita started working at the Spoon, evening shift. I worked days but we overlapped a few times during the week. I began to relax around her until she gave me the quick glance I thought she had reserved for her kids. All of a sudden I was frightened and totally creeped out. That glance read dark volumes! I was receiving too many bad vibes. When it happened, I realized why she was able to so charmingly control and manipulate her little gentlemen and the little lady, as she called her kids. I felt she was dangerous and when we'd made that eye contact, she knew I saw her dark side. For a moment I had a helpless, sinking feeling. Later, I felt amused when she talked on, said she had once owned a Porsche. She didn't know what model or anything, so I told her Boss had been a Porsche mechanic in a previous lifetime and I was sure he could tell us.

"Unbelievable!" I thought. "No way! Not only is she low class but how the heck could she possibly fit behind the wheel of a Porsche?"

It turned out that a friend of her brother's had sold it to her for $100.00, years ago. It needed lots of work, had been in a wreck. She must have been thinner then.

Rita started working her evenings. She said she liked keeping busy after she got the kids to bed, and her next door neighbor kept an eye on them. Seemed like a good deal to me.

After Rita began working at the Spoon, things began to be different. Our kitchen tools were never where they used to be, in places where rational people would keep them. Bowl scrapers sat by the oven, the meat grinder was now by the freezer, which was odd, since we hardly used it. Under the counter where it used to be were now bags of chocolate and boxes of candy-making ingredients. Pot holders were by the ice cream machine now. The cheese began to live over by the grill window. Almost everything had been moved around for no purpose I could see.

When I complained to Boss, his reply was, "That's where Rita can reach and I think those are good places for the stuff."

A new, safer stool appeared and I was glad. We had all stood on the rickety step-ladder for weeks, very carefully, reaching for items on the upper shelves. I heard Boss call the new one, "Rita's stool."

"Why not, 'our stool,' Boss?"

He said, "I couldn't watch Rita up there on that old ladder. Imagine her falling through the floor, getting hurt."

I suddenly felt resentful! Didn't Boss care if his lover fell off the step-ladder and broke her neck or at least a foot? Seems like everything was "Rita, Rita, Rita!"

One weekend, cheese sandwiches were made a different way and it turned out that it was Rita's way.

"God, Boss," I said. "How come we do everything Rita's way now, after so long?"

"Rita is the new Night Manager and this is how we're doing things now!" Boss was irritated. "She's a good worker and very conscientious."

I stammered, "When did Rita become the Night Manager?" I was stunned. I couldn't believe how angry, even jealous, I felt!

Boss said, "I made her Night Manager a few days ago. She's a good worker and I feel secure about the Spoon at night when she's in charge."

"I know that! I trained the woman myself ...!" I was trying not to get hysterical.

Boss patted my butt to try and make things right. He said, "Dad wants me for the week before Labor Day, again, so you can take over for me while I'm gone. That better? You can even do the pay-roll for me." He gave me a hug and I took a deep breath, calmer now. I didn't like that scene at all. I hated the feelings I had.

I remembered Rita Junkin's chocolate candies one day when Boss mentioned that Rita's dream was to have a candy store of her own.

I thought to myself, "Good Luck!" Well, at least she had a dream ... but how the hell could she pull off a real candy store? I was starting to keep my mouth shut about Rita more and more. Boss just got defensive when I talked about her. It seemed to me that she had totally snowed Boss. She was manipulating him to the max.

I began hitting my funny bone, my right elbow, on the sharp stainless steel corners of the warming bins under the heat lamps. A week or so later my arm was so sore I could hardly slice a hot dog.

The hundredth time I hit the corner, I yelled out loud, "Jesus! Does that ever hurt! Why do I keep smashing my goddamned elbow on that thing all of a sudden? My right arm is almost paralyzed! Ow-w-w-w!"

Boss replied, "Oh ... I moved the island out a foot or two so Rita could get by easier."

"But ... but ... but ..." I said. I couldn't argue with Boss anymore or give myself any credence, especially as far as Rita was concerned. I told Boss my fears about her but he wouldn't listen. I sounded like a bitch, even to myself, and every time I mentioned Rita's name, Boss just got more defensive. I remembered the darkness behind her eyes.

At the height of the summer, only a week or two later, Boss and I were getting ready for work when he said, "Partner and I are thinking about giving everyone raises except for you. You're part of the family, you know. Maybe later, if there's money."

"I don't believe you're actually saying this! May I ask why? I'm a hard worker who cares about the business more than any of the others! Why shouldn't I get a raise too? Is Rita getting another raise? Her second since she became Night Manager? Is Lazy Fod getting one? What the hell is wrong with me?"

"Well ... you get other benefits," he said. Then seeing my puzzled and astonished expression, he continued, "Well ... we do go out to dinner, movies. Rita says we seem to go out a lot. The Play, you know ..."

"Hey, wait a minute, Boss. Those so-called perks were never presented as 'business expenses!' If they were, you could have written me off!" I felt rage! "Is Rita getting another raise, too?"

"Well ... yes. She's so conscientious and hard working, I feel good leaving the Spoon in her hands at night."

What went through my mind was that I'd worked for Partner and Boss a long time and had a right to a raise, just like every one else.

Meanwhile, almost speechless by what he'd said, I stammered, "But ... but ... but ..." I couldn't believe Rita was getting two raises in the month she'd worked at the Spoon and now she was getting another! I couldn't believe Boss was being so manipulated by the fat lady. It was like, ... something's happenin' here and ya don't know what it is, do you Mr. Boss ... As I said before, there was nothing more I could say about what I felt and saw. Boss looked at me as though I was nuts and I actually wondered for a minute that perhaps I was! I felt as though I was losing my mind. I expressed my fears to Boss and he only laughed.

Summer sped on. Rita got her raise along with everyone else except me. I hung on to my good self-image as best I could and told myself it didn't matter. It was all ego stuff and not that important. I knew I was a good worker and that's what counted in the end. I would have quit except I loved Boss and cared about his business. I cared about Partner too. Plus, I really needed the money I was earning for school.

Boss told Rita that she could sell her chocolates at the Spoon. She put up a display of chocolate raisin and peanut clusters at the pick-up window and every time she sold one, she pocketed the money. All the money.

More and more things were kept where "Rita finds more convenient." By this time my right elbow was so bad I had to use both hands to pick up the gallon jars of mayonnaise and mustard and ketchup. I could hardly write out the orders. Finally, Rita irritated the other employees as well. We thought it would be funny to have a collection jar for "guessing the weight of the fat lady," but this was only said in jest and the closest secretiveness. Jake and Lazy Fod were starting to be wary of her. I wasn't the only one afraid at the Spoon.

Rita began to let the boys leave work early, telling Boss she could do it better herself. Lazy Fod was practically worthless. He was good doing dishes during rush hour. Jake couldn't stand being there a moment longer than he had to, so he jumped at the chance to leave. I remembered that Rita claimed she was so lonely in the evenings so I couldn't figure out why she preferred to work alone at night. She convinced Boss that she was saving him money, I was sure of it. I watched her.

I watched Rita Junkins surreptitiously because I still could not look at her eyes without feeling uncomfortable and afraid. I hated her for laughing at me and laughing at Boss too. All I could do was try to avoid her eyes when we met. I felt the woman was evil and manipulative, and she and I both knew that Boss wouldn't listen to me or believe me. I was totally powerless.

Often, late at night, lights burned at the Spoon. Occasionally my friends told me they saw Boss working late with Rita. I wasn't jealous of the fat lady, not in the usual sense, that is. What bothered me about the late night activities at the Spoon was that Boss had given Rita three raises and made her the Night Manager. Why the hell did he have to be working there too?

Labor Day approached. Boss went off as planned for his parental visit the week before. I was a little hurt that he left without saying goodbye, but not very surprised, since we had been irritated with each other lately. Oh well, I would see him in a week and we'd both be cooled off by then.

Before Boss left, he gave me instructions about getting the payroll out and ordering food for the busy weekend. We needed hot dogs, mayonnaise, mustard, French fries and ketchup, hot dog rolls and lots of hamburger buns and of course soft ice cream ingredients for the machine. I doubled our regular orders as Boss suggested. Better to have too much. We had plenty of fry-o-later oil, and Farmer Cole had supplied us with bushels of fresh lettuces and tomatoes for the weekend. I put in a special order for crabmeat and clams to Beulah, and, we needed more boxes of haddock. The only thing we didn't seem to need was hamburger.

Labor Day weekend was a huge success despite a thunder storm in the middle of the day, and the fact that Boss hadn't gotten back to help run the place. Both Lazy Fod and Jake reluctantly filled in and we were able to pull it off. Everyone was exhausted and we'd used up practically everything, although Rita sent Jake up to the Joint with 25 pounds of extra ground meat.

Jake dragged his heels up the hill. "Hey Partner, Rita wants to know if you can fit this meat into one of the freezers up here. We're out of room."

Partner took the load and as he was trying to stuff it in to one of the freezer units said, "Did you forget the invoice again, Jake?"

"Uh-h-h, Rita didn't give it to me, Partner. Geez, I guess she can't find it … that's what she said, anyway."

Partner and I were getting annoyed with Boss, leaving it all up to us. I got the payroll out.

Boss and I had been having a loving relationship for quite a while. I didn't usually worry about him or wonder what he was up to. He always had projects to do and people to see, but I waited patiently for a card, then less patiently for a phone call.

I asked Partner if he'd heard from Boss, and he said, "No, I haven't but he'd better get his ass back here soon. I want him to help me close down the Joint now that the big weekend is over!"

I asked Rita if she'd heard anything from Boss, if she knew when he was coming back. She claimed, "I know nothin', except he said to keep the place open 'til he gets back." I was done being surprised, but a strike of fear cut quickly through my chest. She was so menacing! Glancing at her from the corner of my eye, I swear she looked bigger.

Lazy Fod and Jake both almost forgot to pick up their final pay checks but they did eventually and then they drifted off for the winter months to collect unemployment. As far as I was concerned, I was done with the weekends and days and I had to get on up to school, just as Boss and I had decided.

I called Boss's dad and I was surprised that he hadn't seen him. He said Boss hadn't shown up for his visit. I wondered if he thought we should call the cops or something but he said, "You know Boss. He probably took the opportunity to visit some college buddies. You go on up to school. I'll decide what to do soon and let you know."

The Night Manager continued to run the Spoon, selling only burgers and chocolates, finally. I later heard that with each day that passed, more and more different chocolates appeared by the windows. Lights burned on into the nights. I heard there were chocolate bunnies and cats, humans and monkeys, chocolate clusters, with or without raisins, chocolate squares and ovals, triangles and drops, chocolate butter crunchies and chocolate fingers. And before the eyes of the town, slowly, slowly, so slowly that no one noticed a change, the Spoon became the Chocolate Spoon.

Mrs. Roosevelt and Mrs. Raven

Deborah Wedgwood Marshall

Mrs. Roosevelt, dressed in chocolate brown chiffon with a matching silk shawl, and wide Panama hat shielding her eyes, velvet collar askew, peacock feathers winking and gleaming in the April sun, staggered, with her sister, up the path to Great Aunt Pierce's house. Mrs. Raven wore tulle of a reddish color, green velvet cuffs and collar, and an embroidered green shawl around her small shoulders. Her hat was also a Panama, with a crumbling brim. They both wore cast-off shoes. Mrs. Roosevelt's were black slings from the 20's and her sister's were stadium pumps, last worn by her mum at the 1939 World's Fair in Jamaica, New York only a month before she was born. Mrs. Roosevelt, two-and-a-half years older and a little taller, stood on tiptoes to reach the doorbell. They giggled nervously and slapped their hands over their mouths as they heard the slow tread inside the house getting closer.

Aunt Pierce opened the door slowly and, noticing the two ladies, smiled and said, "Why hello, Mrs. Roosevelt and ... Mrs. Raven, is it? I'm glad you could stop in. Please ..." and she held the door aside, gesturing at them to enter. "Would you gir ... umm, ladies like some tea? I've just put the pot on. I was about to have some myself. Won't you please join me?"

Auntie Pierce was tall and "big boned," as Mum would say. She reminded the young ladies of Little Orphan Annie from the comic strip, but instead of yellow hair, Aunt Pierce's was a fluffy, white halo, and instead of round white eyes, Auntie's were round and dark because she always wore dark glasses. She was also much, much bigger.

Mrs. Raven poked her sister surreptitiously in the ribs with her small elbow and murmured to Aunt Pierce, "Peace offerings. We came for peace offerings. We won't have time for tea. Do you have anything for us today?" She blushed and dropped her head as Mrs. Roosevelt interrupted, "Oh, yes, that would be very lovely, Miss Pierce. We'd love to have a cup!" Mrs. Raven was shy with older people and people she didn't know well, and in trying not to be grasping, she sometimes was. She had offered her basket to Aunt Pierce, then pulled it back quickly, with embarrassment.

"Well, good, then! Come into the parlor and have a chair. I will go and get the tea ready, and please, have one of these freshly baked brownies. I made them myself today and I believe it's the recipe that you both like best!" Aunt Pierce walked over to the sideboard where there was a flowered plate piled high with the goodies.

Aunt Pierce left the room and the ladies each grabbed for a favorite brownie. Mrs. Raven, whose name was Ethel, liked the corners best and Mrs. Roosevelt, who was Eleanor, always took the ones in the center. Although they could have eaten four brownies apiece, each timidly took a second, and, glancing quickly around, each took another and dropped it into her basket. Ethel's basket was an ancient Easter basket that had belonged to her Mum, when Mum was small. Eleanor's was also old, probably older, and was a sewing basket from China, from one of her Little Auntie's world tours.

Ethel said, "This is so much fun! Auntie Pierce sure makes the best brownies!"

"Sh-h-h-h! Shut up, Annie. She'll hear and know who we are," said Mrs. Roosevelt, whose real name was Maggie.

Aunt Pierce came back into the parlor with the silver tea service, the pot steaming hot. She asked the girls in turn if they would like "one lump or two." Then she added milk to each cup without asking. After all, the girls had taken tea with Aunt Pierce many times before.

Eleanor began chatting, explaining what they were doing, "For the war effort, Miss Pierce. We are working hard today collecting peace offerings. We have many more stops to make!"

Aunt Pierce offered her another brownie, "Wouldn't you like another, Mag ... I mean, Eleanor. Ethel? Just one more, and I will go and see what I have. Yes, I think I have some things for your effort." The girls had had enough by then and they both refused. Ethel remembered they had more goodies in their baskets.

"Thank you Miss Pierce. The more items we can get, the more money we can raise for the war effort and "bring the boys home" as Mum would say."

Aunt Pierce left the room again and returned shortly, her arms filled with interesting looking objects. "Mrs. Raven, I think these will do you nicely." And into her basket, Aunt Pierce placed a leather coin purse, a dusty bouquet of fake flowers, and a shimmering hat.

Ethel Raven was too shy to scrutinize the hat thoroughly in front of Aunt Pierce, but she was just as curious as she was shy, and she couldn't wait to leave so she could study it properly. She murmured, "Thank you, Miss Pierce ... and the war effort thanks you too!"

Then Ethel watched as Aunt Pierce gently deposited a colorfully painted plaster swan into her sister's basket, along with an old medal of some sort and a dusty book. She was thinking it must have been Uncle Pierce's stuff, before he was "gathered," as Mum would say. Aunt Pierce said sadly, "Uncle Horace earned that medal in WW One. He wrote this little book during his second tour abroad, before he was shot. It should bring a pretty penny at the sale."

Ethel wanted to reach out and touch the plaster swan but she restrained herself as Eleanor said, "Thank you, Miss Pierce. You will find your reward in heaven!"

The young ladies bowed, then curtsied and made their exit, trailing satin ribbons and feathers. Once they had said their good-byes and Auntie Pierce had closed her door, they started running down the path, losing shoes as they went. With skirts held high, they threw the shoes into their baskets with their treasures and ran down the street, around the corner, past the cemetery to the grove of oak trees bordering the back of the Town Green, where they flopped on the grass and rolled around, all out of breath, laughing.

Annie and Maggie knew that all their Mother's friends thought it was so cute of them to dress up and go from door to door asking for "peace offerings." The girls didn't know what it all meant, really. They had heard the grown-ups talk a lot about "peace" and the "war effort" and Victory gardens and WW Two. All these things were why Daddy was away, but at ages seven and nine-and-a-half they thought it was a good game.

Annie sat up first and took the strange hat out from her basket and looked at it closely. It was a turban, the color of dark shimmering turquoise. Later she would learn that the color was Mediterranean Blue, not turquoise at all. The turban was covered with a silky veil of the same color, and underneath it were sparkles that looked like tiny silver fish swimming in the sea, but when she lifted the veil there were just rhinestones and sequins sewn in a spiral.

Maggie saw it then and grabbed the hat, jamming it on her head. "I'm a fortune teller!" She jumped up and hopped around and around, laughing, the hat well down over her ears.

Annie, surprised by her sister's sudden action, yelled, "NO NO NO! Give it back!" She jumped at her sister and knocked her to the ground. She took the hat back and shoved it into her Easter basket. No longer surprised and angry, she said more softly, "Maggie, let me see your swan." She was startled at her outburst and the feelings she'd had!

"No, you creep. You won't let me see your hat so you can't see my swan. I was going to show it to you, but not now!" Maggie jumped up, and holding her basket close to her chest ran toward home.

Annie sighed, "I guess we won't be making any more stops today, after all." Disappointed, she followed her sister. She decided the swan didn't look that interesting, anyway. It looked like a cheap plaster statue from the Fair. She wouldn't admit it to herself, but she really did want to hold it and study it. She thought of offering to trade the hat for the swan, but the thought was fleeting.

Maggie had run up to her bedroom and put the plaster swan on the shelf with the rest of her peace offerings, after she had studied the colorful bird. She was mostly interested in horses and horse stuff, and had quite a collection, including an old stirrup, two or three little porcelain horse statues, a frayed horse hair riding whip, a kerchief printed with cowboy lariats and lassoes and horse silhouettes. Someone had given her an old portrait of Whirlaway. She had a dozen *Horse and Rider* magazines which were at least 20 years old.

In her room, Annie scrutinized her shelf of objects which she'd collected around the neighborhood with her sister, in the name of peace. There were old books of tickets from the Criterion Theatre. She had many necklaces and bracelets, a pack of Pinochle cards. Her favorite was the gold painted wishbone given to her by Mrs. Adams down the street when she was seven years old. "That must have been a hundred years ago!" Annie thought. Her collection also included several tiny decorated boxes and a large woven basket that was made by the Passamaquoddy Indians in Maine; ribbons, crocheted doilies and three lace cuffs; millefiori beads from Venice, Italy; and a belt of green stones that her mother said were jade. Someone, she couldn't remember who, had given her a ratty old stuffed tiger. She took the turban from her basket and placed it on the tiger's head and she put her extra brownie under the tiger so Maggie wouldn't know where it was, just in case. Her mother called the girls for supper.

As usual, Maggie and Annie ate their evening meal in the little hallway just outside the kitchen. Mum had made shepherd's pie, with fresh cooked spinach on the side, and carrot and celery sticks. Annie ate Maggie's mashed potato topping and Maggie ate Annie's ground lamb filling. They both loved spinach but were not interested in the carrots and celery so they stuffed them into the big knothole that was under the table where the vegetables disappeared from sight and mind.

Mum came and stood by the table, as they ate their spinach, to ask about the day's activities. "And how is Aunt Pierce today? Did you ask if her arthritis is better?"

"Oh, no! We forgot!" said Maggie. "But she did give us some good peace offerings."

"She made those good brownies again," Annie slurped through her spinach.

"Yes, Aunt Pierce certainly does have the best recipe in the world. I should ask her to make a few dozen for the sale on Saturday ... what is this, Wednesday?

"That's too soon, Mum," Annie blurted out. "I haven't looked at all my stuff yet!"

"Now, Mrs. Raven, you know that you have been collecting for the war effort. Maybe ... but maybe, you could each pick out one special thing to keep. I'm sure no one would mind."

Before bed, the girls sat together in Maggie's room. Annie had finally been allowed to hold the plaster swan and she really wanted it. She asked Maggie, "Let's trade, OK? I'll give you my old, old wishbone and you give me your plaster swan."

"No, you're nuts! But I might trade it for that hat, even though it's just part of some cheesy fortune teller's costume. Auntie Pierce probably got it at a junk store!"

"It is not! You're stupid! Good bye!" Annie bounded out of Maggie's room and into her own, slamming the door. Her sister was stupid, even though she was older. "Well, tomorrow..." Annie thought. She'd ask Maggie to trade the swan for the wishbone and a pair of earrings. If she wouldn't do it, then maybe, just maybe, she'd trade the hat for the swan. "Hm-m-m … if Mum really lets us each keep one thing, then I'll be able to play with both things, especially if Mag keeps the swan ... and I keep the hat ... I'll have to talk to her about it in the morning ..."

After Mum had kissed the girls good night, sung songs and tucked them in with a kiss, she closed each door. Annie reached for the hat and, even in the dark room, she could imagine little fish swimming through a dark ocean at night with stars far overhead sparkling. She soon fell asleep with her treasure clasped to her breast.

Somewhere, We Must Survive

After we came home from the funeral
home, they made a black and white photo
of us (somewhere, we must survive)
arranged up the front hall stairs,
our father at the top, dignified,
holding us together, with our mother,
more or less, by his side, unfamiliar off-
center, peering over our heads into the flash,
her mouth a slash, taut, hospital-cornered.

As we slept she sketched the Alps,
the Himalayas, onto the bare north face
of our living room wall. It took weeks.
With charcoal chalks she jabbed sheer peaks
at the ceiling — aqua heaven — and under these
arranged nether clouds thinning to spent
streams in the blue corners of her room.

There's another photo of us before
that wall, leaning against her
plump (re-centered) knees, crowding
her billowy arms, ten bud mouths smiling.
In the foreground our brother
floats — an anemic yogi —
in his favorite Hawaiian shirt, grinning
because he's wearing pineapples and
palm leaves in the Himalayas.

—*Jacqueline Michaud*

Hung Jury

None of us was excused, assigned seating,
and it was no picnic — let me tell you —
watching the twitch of the accused, his dry
mouth guzzling water throughout the cross-
examination, no lark deciding
who was lying more — him, his ex-girlfriend
in her third trimester, or her first born,

a toddler learning new words. "Life sucks,"
one juror beefed whose wife had made a pork
roast over the weekend and it was his
"personal goal" to return home before
Survivor came on. The foreman, in Sales
for a local Dodge dealership aimed his
laser at a board on which he had chalked:

Motive … Means … Opportunity. "You watch
too many cop shows," Porky groused, as a
housewife, furious with the woman judge
who would not let her knit during the trial
("She's making me a hostile witness?"), called
the defendant's ex-girlfriend "a low-life
slut, and besides, what man in his right mind

would let a teething child do that? It's sick!"
The bailiff took ten orders for take-out —
turkey, tuna, chicken-salad on rye.
Five past eight ticked the big analog clock
high on the wall over the brown locked door,
just like in third grade. In fat block letters
we printed our verdicts on little squares

of paper the foreman had passed around.
He liked playing boss — unfolding, tallying,
ticking us off. Seven times we did that,
and after each round he'd frown, puff his chest

out and bark, "OK, have it your way," then
drag us back to the transcript, trying not
to shout, "Come on, which one of you is it?"

Two years later, the acquitted was back
in The News under District Police Beat,
the word "alleged" misspelled in the headline.

—*Jacqueline Michaud*

The Ardent Dog

The ardent dog ached for squirrels, every day,
his passion. Around red maples,
through the gazebo, into the prickle bush
they teased, their puff tails twitching.

You just wait, just wait!
he'd tremble,
hot eyes gleaming
into the red rustle of leaves.

One day, when he wasn't doing anything
about squirrels, but lolling on his back
under a dogwood in blossom: a loud crack
and sudden clatter of twigs.

He looked up, red tongue relaxed
in the seasonal heat, as a full-grown
squirrel fell through the leaves, smack
into his mouth.

For a small while he quivered, muzzle apulse
with the weight of his passion,
then did what no dog ought to,
when something wonderful, something

he's been scouting all his backyard
life is delivered — blood, bones,
pelt and fragrance, had them all
and spit them out.

—Jacqueline Michaud

A Safe Place

Elisabeth Reed

It was just turning dark when Ginger came through the back door of the kitchen. She put her groceries down on the counter, where her husband, Peter, was reorganizing the silverware in the drawer. "You should make sure the knives go one way and the spoons and forks alternate in another," he said. His body was tense.

She laughed.

"Yeah, and Hello."

"Hello." He closed the drawer and left the room.

She started to put the bag of brown rice on the hutch when she caught a glimpse of herself in the mirror. She was forty-five years old, with lots of thick red hair. Most redheads had freckles as part of the bargain, but Ginger's face was smooth and round. Her eyes were large and clear amber. As she looked closer into the mirror she saw two strong lines extending from the sides of her nose downward towards her chin. She didn't recognize the person looking back at her. The face was tired and drawn. During her yearly check up, her doctor had voiced concern about her appearance. When Ginger had tried to kid with her and said maybe she should try some collogen or botox, the woman had looked her straight in the eye and suggested that the two deep creases between her brows were from anger.

Her husband didn't answer when she opened the door slowly and walked into his library. He was staring at the floor, his face pale with sadness. It confused her so she began the timid game of engagement. "I really had a good time at the Dubinskys'. They have such a beautiful house," she said eyeing him. "You would have appreciated their taste."

"You know I hate that word." He took off his glasses and rubbed his eyes.

She smiled at him. "I'm sorry, I'm making it sound like a cliché, but I know you love beautiful wood, and their fireplace is a Mackintosh design in oiled cherry. It's …"

"I don't care," He said.

Ginger leaned against the curtains. The silk liner was cool between her fingers. Outside the snow glowed through the street lamp. Two of the neighbors' children walked by, bundled up. Closing her eyes, she tried to remember what it felt like to be happy. She thought about her drive home today. That afternoon she had driven along Rt. 3 from Wiscasset. The warm March light encouraged her to feel she might be strong enough to reach him. "I don't expect you to care," she began, turning to face him, "I thought you loved textures, like ..."

He was angry now, "Give it a rest, Ginger, are you listening? Do you even know I'm here?"

A shiver of fear made its way up her spine. "How could I miss. You're taking up all the oxygen in the room."

His tone was malignant. "You know I'm not interested in those people. You're trying to drag me through some new door." He began to sift through a file of papers on his desk. It was a cool dismissal.

She squeezed her eyes shut and started again. "I'm trying to include you."

"Don't bother." He cut her off, opening his computer.

She stood in the middle of the room, wondering how a library full of books could feel so lonely. "Maybe it's because all the doors here are closed," she whispered and turned to leave.

"This is who I am, Ginger," he said loudly. She put her fingers over her ears, and started back to the kitchen. "I'm working for some kind of peace and quiet."

"You're working towards separation. That's quiet." Then he was up and in front of her pulling her hands down to her sides. "Don't you take your guilt out on me!" she yelled at him.

He stopped and looked down at her. She couldn't breathe. Everything he felt was in his face. "'People shouldn't have to live like this." His voice was strained.

She looked up into his face. "Like what? Have you done something?"

For the next three hours, she listened to his confession. She had instinctively known it even before he began his defense. He said, "I've been in agony for months."

"Months," she repeated, shaking her head. "Who is she this time?"

His face went beet red with anger. "You're making this harder than it has to be."

"I asked you a question. I'm entitled to an answer," Ginger said, tears starting down her cheeks.

"Listen Ginger, the last person I would ever want to hurt is you."

"Oh please, you're sounding like daytime television."

When he had exhausted his self pity, he mumbled a quick confession about a woman at the hospital, an oncology intern, brilliant. It sounded to her like he was practicing a speech. He might as well have been standing in front of the microphone at one of his award dinners. The handsome doctor hypnotizes them with the agony of the sinning husband. It had that kind of performance level.

She sat at the kitchen table, holding her face with both hands. His voice was contrite. "You've always been able to get your strength from people. Maybe you should go back to massage school. You're so good with anyone who's damaged."

"Apparently not."

He hung his head and shook it from side to side. "Shame makes liars of us all."

She got up, went over to where he sat, and crouched in front of his face. "Don't bother to include me, Peter."

"Oh yes, you're in that group too. Even as the faithful wife, you have your part."

"I don't believe in that theory that everything that happens between us is a 50-50 responsibility. I'm not the one with the habit of leaving this marriage."

"Well then what part do you feel you do play in all of this?" She didn't answer. He sighed and looked out the window at the snow.

"You're not this big a loser, tell me you're not."

"I can't talk to you when you get like this," he said, turning away from her.

"This? This is what betrayal looks like."

He took his coat and walked out the back door. She heard the car's engine. The room was spinning and she couldn't remember what they'd decided. Running down the steps, she waved at him to stop as he pulled out of the garage. The snow was coming down in big soft flakes and he made her stand and wait. The window slid down. She was crying now. "Will you just come back inside?"

He shrugged his shoulders, "I can't." Then he drove away.

Sleepless and exhausted, Ginger walked around the house all night, finishing their old arguments and making points he wasn't there to hear. She was alternately furious and devastated and kept losing track. The dogs followed her from room to room and pushed their noses into her hand whenever she sat down. Looking around their home, all she could see was sharp colors and dust. "I've got to leave. I've got to think," she said.

At dawn, it was clear to her that he was not coming back. She knew he wouldn't have risked being recognized in one of the hotels in town. That left only one place he could be, and that made her feel homely. She walked down into the empty kitchen to make herself some coffee, but couldn't face it. Sitting on their bed, she cried and scribbled a note, "I'm going somewhere safe," and signed it. Organizing what she needed was exhausting. She pulled on her hiking clothes, and threw together some dog food and trail supplies for herself in her back pack. The sun was bright yellow against the windshield when she drove past the Hospital. She couldn't see his car, so she turned around and drove through the parking lot. There was no sign of him.

Gripping the steering wheel, she went over his gloomy story. He had explained how this affair was different from the last time, as if that made it more worthy. He'd droned on, defending his adultery. "You and I have been stuck in a symbiotic relationship. There's too much attachment." Where'd he pick that one up? She recalled his penitence was half-hearted, even menacing. He had forbidden her to engage in any gossip that might threaten his practice. She drove past the beautiful pristine Maine homes and wondered if those snow covered houses held the same kind of trauma and deceit.

The last time he'd lied to her, one of her friends had told her she'd seen him in Boston. He had been nuzzling some woman in a corner of a restaurant. Ginger had thought the whole thing about running after someone else was confusing. She tried to convince him to go into therapy with her. This exposed his venomous side. "I am a doctor, Ginger. I don't need one."

Passing the tiny old post office, she longed for a friend, someone with whom she could sit and have coffee. But there wasn't anyone. He had always found a way to burlesque some defining quality in all of her friends. He seemed to expect she would eventually forgive his criticisms and treachery, as if they had made a silent contract. They were way out of balance.

Most of what everyone said about Ginger had to do with her sense of humor, but it was her gentleness that built up his pediatric practice. She caught herself remembering something back at the office she'd forgotton to mention.

She had been his assistant since the first year out of his internship, and his wife for fifteen years after that. It horrified her to realize all that common experience was made a burlesque, the inevitable ending in one night. Then the old longing for him would start and she was disgusted by her own weakness.

When she turned off the highway at noon, she was four hours away from their house. She looked over at her dog, Ruddy, a big blue heeler, sitting straight in the passenger seat. He paid close attention to the road. He was so constant, it made her cry again. "I need a guard dog," she said softly. He dove between the seats for his toy. Ears flat back along his rounded head, his tail churned his body back and forth in one constant wiggle. His snow colored sister Loli was curled up against Ginger's stomach.

They left the car off Sugar Hill, and slogged in through the new snow. It was quiet in the forest but the wind caught the tops of the trees and pushed them to swing and crack. Ginger was tall and strong but she'd been watching the scales tip heavier in the last three years, and now the awkwardness of her balance made maneuvering slippery. Every once in awhile she sank through the crusty cover up to the knee. This afternoon, she was in no mood for caution. The dogs vaulted up through clouds of spray and started mock battles. Ginger watched, numb. It occurred to her that they were her only link to joy. Loli had short legs and couldn't keep up the pace so she fell in behind Ginger.

After two hours of workout, they finally broke out of the woods and fell to rest on the bank, where the Dead River rounds a bend. The clouds were moving fast. Ice was jammed up between the pine islands that stretched across to the other side.

She scanned the opposite meadows to find the high triangle of trees and their cabin. Every summer her husband chose to join his physician friends on Long Island for their fancy fundraisers, and, happily, Ginger spent ten days at his family's cabin with the dogs. She winced, remembering how each night, she was so eager to hear his voice on the phone. She was attracted to people by the timbre of their voices. He said it was her Irish. This time of year, the phones were turned off and she was relieved. No one knew where she was.

The bridge was still rotted out in a three-year downstream lean because the spring floods had been unable to carry the old bollards out. The ice islands looked yellow underwater. Arched against her pack on a hardened drift, with the dogs trotting around sniffing, she thought about trust. She closed her eyes and breathed in the silence. A shiver of cold made her tap her hands together to revive the feeling in her fingers. She looked down at her boots and wondered about going back, but the woods looked ghostly and the light would soon be grey. The wind had dropped, leaving only white wildness. She got up, called to the dogs, and moved slowly ahead over the embankment. The snow was hard on the top of the ice near the edge of the river, so Ginger moved forward quickly.

The first loud crack went skipping under the ice about fifteen feet off to her left. It was impossible to tell where it had started. She stopped and looked quickly at the dogs, nervous on the bridge above her. When the second break sounded immediately underneath her, Ginger lost her balance. She flung her hands out, but the deep snap under her boots hurled her backwards and she hit the ice on the side of her face.

The dogs began barking and running back and forth. Ginger dug in her heels and thrust herself towards the shore. The thick ice slabs folded in, and she went under. When her foot hit the bottom, she pushed up through the water, gasping for air. Loli came off the bridge, skidded past, and disappeared underwater. The little dog bobbed up with a worried look on her face and floundered. Striking her paws high on the water, she fought to turn herself upstream. Then Ruddy came off the bridge in a diver's arc and landed squarely on top his sister, pushing her back under the ice. They surfaced growling, both of them flailing until they swung around where the current pulled them out into the center of the river.

Ginger launched herself towards them in the black water. She tried to remember how deep it was, but her mind wouldn't work. Somewhere her glasses had fallen off, but her vision was crystal clear. As she was carried out into the main channel, everything felt frozen except her eyes. The cold belonged to another world, until the dogs smashed up against her skull. It felt icy and hard. She screamed at them, "Move off!"

Ruddy began swimming for the other bank, but the little dog couldn't make it. He was straining to pull himself up on the ice bank, when Loli flailed into Ginger and they rolled over again in the flood. Ginger's heavy boots pulled them deeper into the water as she tried to turn the terrified dog into her chest. Loli raked at Ginger's face as they rounded the bend and snagged up on a frozen tree trunk stuck between the rocks. Loli got her back foot caught in the canopy of Ginger's hood and twisted away onto a rock netted with frozen twigs. Ginger couldn't get her weight to heave out of the pull of the water. She felt herself losing grip. The branches snapped and she sank back.

Pushing her arms out in a stroke, she tried to kick again, but her body was remote and heavy. Everything was moving slowly. She sank underwater. She could see her hair in front of her face in a dim flash of light and green bubbles. The water filled up her nose and throat.

There was no memory of climbing through the water when her head punched through a thin piece of ice, only that the daylight blinded her. Ruddy swam into her. He kept trying to catch her wrist in his mouth. When he finally had a grip, he turned, swimming hard. But Ginger's strength was gone and her body swept away into the rapids and down a long narrow drop. At the bottom, above the rushing water, the river waste was mashed over the fallen rocks. She stuck there, staring up through the trees.

Ginger was dreaming about water, like music, coming closer. Turning her head against her frozen collar, she saw the blackened timbers sticking out of the water. She pushed her fingers against the mangled brush and looked down to see her foot sticking straight up at an odd angle. Muscle by muscle she lowered herself onto the first log. Trying to steady her balance along the big tree on her back, she grabbed at the splintered half branches, but they kept snapping underneath her. Out where the water had stripped away any extra brush, she struggled to stop shaking and lay there watching the light fade.

The big dog floundered in the shallows and finally pulled himself back up on the bank. He scrambled up river towards his sister who lay on her side, about thirty feet away. He nipped at her. She didn't move. He circled in, growling. Grabbing her lower back leg in his teeth, he shook it and then bit down. Loli's muscles contracted until the hair on her shoulders stood on end. She snarled at him, rolled over and pulled herself up on her belly. He left her there and dashed along the treeline where the willow roots hung out from the bank.

In the distance, Ginger heard both dogs barking hoarsely. The air looked blurry. Each part of her body felt unreachable. She stared at the puffy images. They scratched her face until she recognized the shore willows. She had made it to where the tree's roots stuck back into the riverbank. It seemed an endless amount of time before she inched her way off the log. Lying on the snow and ice, she began to feel a curious warmth. The dogs sniffed around her face until she pulled herself up onto her knees and peered up at the speck of a cabin. It was too far away.

Somehow, Ruddy found a trail in that general direction. Dumb from cold, Ginger stumbled after him, up through the drifts. It was maddening to go back and forth across the rocks and ledges. She couldn't control her body's shaking. She kept needing to lie down in the snow. But Loli would flop down next to her and wait, panting.

Her hands were cut up, so she couldn't touch the ground to steady her body anymore without crying out. When at last she slid backwards down a high embankment, Loli came through the air behind her. The little dog scambled off Ginger's back and began to lick the side of her face. It scraped and burned like tough grade sandpaper. "Stop it," Ginger begged and rolled over to cover her face. When she opened her eyes, the cabin porch was less than a hundred feet away.

The front door lock was frozen, and Ginger cursed the world that needed them. Her fingers stuck to the metal. She twisted the dial in its housing. She kicked at it with her foot until the metal arm separated from the cylinder. Once inside, she crashed around like a bear, upsetting the shelves. Inside the fireplace, the logs were set, left by hunters. She sank down on the stone hearth, opened her jacket and stuck her hands under both of her armpits. They felt like blocks of ice. It was unbelievably painful to strike the edge of the wooden match box, again and again. Very slowly she rolled up one of the old newspapers. She twice blew out the match's tiny flame. When the paper did catch, it burned her.

The dogs moved in close to her under an old Indian blanket while the sticks hissed and began to throw out heat. They glowed as she banked in two more logs. Her clothes were so wet and crusted, she had to scrape them off her skin and it burned. Some wool pajamas were left in her husband's bureau. Supplies for a tender trip never taken. Her hands were trembling too hard to work the big plastic buttons. Ginger tried to make her mind work, to feel her body again, where it was cut and bruised.

She awakened to the fire's pink light in the cabin. She lowered the blanket off her head, and turned her back to the fire. Her eyes were swollen and sticky. She crawled over to the long window and squinted through the iced glass. The faintest crescent moon was rising across the sky. Below, the snow fields were white and grim. For the first time she felt separate from her husband. His betrayal was clear enough to her, and uncomplicated like a childhood wound. Marriage had separated them for longer than the illusion of holding them together, and only rations of love had remained. All the old possibilities were gone. The contract was over. Studying the cabin, she saw it had only the bare essentials, but it was full of her own history, and the one safe place where she could begin.

Forsythia with Snow

I am irked by snow
Dallying
On the lawn, inclined
By the tall forsythia.

It is May, the bevy
Of specificity
And premise of leaves.

I consider
The eddying, swept decorum
Of other snow
And lax lawn,

The window, a mixed sky,

Yard
With veins
Of disinclination, and nooks.

In unmelting disregard
It stands,

In white embrace,

Protecting, with a sprig
Of accent,

A figment of gain.

I sit
Or presume to sit

An eye
Level with
Accommodation,

A gesture
Signed
Of intended benediction.

We are not equals
At work

In
The branched
Frost

Of creation,

Plunged
In it,

Blazing
A discourse.

There
Stretches
The distinction.

An image
Of snow

Construing spring —

Then,
A shudder.

The figure not us
Moves

In a wilderness
Of abeyance.

—Stephen Rifkin

Of Irises

So much is framed and unsaid
In language

Where light is published
The eye amended

In the newspapers

In a garden
At dusk

Blades stem and bud or now stars
Bluish and blush

Divide misstatements equally and meanings

Interpose
Life is fleeting

Vaguely over walks and ubiquitous trees
Some crux the more a sense of wounds

Overfelt doubtless
On paper

Between each cut slim flower

A betrayal minute
As you sip and while you read

In the space
of trials

After hard quiet

Some process or the dark news
Altering phrases you suspect

Concerning irises and creation itself

—*Stephen Rifkin*

When Women Grow Old

When women grow old and stop being women,
they grow beards on their chins
Strindberg, *The Father*

These jutting hairs on my chin
seem to arrive overnight
like the startling two-inch gray one
I find growing from one ear lobe.

At her mirror, plucking,
shaping her brows like Dietrich,
permed hair still brown,
my mother's image persists.
Not yet old when she died,
too young to sit in the shade and spin
home remedies for others,
she could not cure herself —
the stone in her breast
weighting her dreams.

There is so little left:
her few paintings, a silver wedding ring,
birth certificate in safe deposit.
I accidentally gave away her tweezers
years ago to a stranger whose house burned;
packaged them with good intentions
and other odds and ends from my vanity
and dresser drawers; a duplicate
I thought then, of no sentimental value.

—Norma Voorhees Sheard

Old Salt Water Farm

for Nancy Hodermarsky

Daylilies, delphinium and lavender
crowd against humps of granite.
The wind is swift today,
stamping a path from bay and meadow
through Nancy's gardens.
Its feisty salt breath
makes the old asparagus fronds tremble.
Stalks slip from their holding rings,
their green tops, feather dusters
with nothing to do.

—Norma Voorhees Sheard

Radiance

for Barbara Luhks,
died 23 July 2001

This is the hour of boats at anchor
when low sun paints their sides
as though from within.

At the window, wine in hand,
we celebrate the end of day.
To the east one ridge of cloud

violet and smoke, pale white.
Except for a loon's meditation
and the ripple of outgoing tide

all is hushed.
One boat glides with grace
beyond Basket and Sturdevand,

then makes ready to tack.
When we look again, it has already
rounded the point.

—Norma Voorhees Sheard

Zen Garden

for Gayle and Dan Hadley

'Happiness is not made, but given.'
—Robert Farnsworth, "Uses of the Cedar" *Honest Water*

Red-turned leaves of azalea.
Granite. Ivory and red pebbles.
Beachwood, stripped clean.
On the pond the first skin of ice.

Reluctant to relinquish its voice
one cricket, its glissando
repeated. Repeated.

Stone Buddha idles
at the wood line.
A trickle of sunlight
illuminates the way.

—*Norma Voorhees Sheard*

You Called Me What?

they are the ones who call you
Dear and *Dearie* and *Hon* and *Love*
the chubby waiter
with boredom as his middle name

the woman at the checkout counter
who scans the goods
and gives you change
all the time her mind

consumed with her daughter
who's about to be evicted
with two kids and a dog
and no other place available

and she says *Dearie* like
the gum-snapping teen
at the other checkout
says *ya know*

it rolls off their tongues
like dog sweat on a summer day
drips here drips there
just a figure of speech

a little bit sweet
a little bit sour

—Julian A. Waller

Just Before Winter

for Irene and Richard

far too soon comes Autumn
and squirrels scurry around
gather their hordes
of acorns and nuts
hide here bury there
caches in so many places
you wonder how they could
remember them all

and right on cue Irene begins
the mindless task
to stack the wood
mindless is what she calls it
but it's something she loves to do
the repetitive bend-lift-stack
the rhythm – even after a fashion –
the grace
as one ordered pile grows
and one disordered pile shrinks
to nothingness

the simple zenness of the
here-to-there motion repeated
and repeated
a manual cleansing of summer
now quickly turning brown
a cleansing down to the very
whiteness of winter

some time in the deepest dark
of a winter's eve
dislodging yet another log from the pile
halved or quartered now dry as bone
she will suddenly smile
and reaching her hand a bit further

she will pick up a few dried rose hips
or a milkweed pod
a snippet of ribbon
a sprig of summer grasses
a well-worn treasured note
that speaks of love
one of the small memories
of a summer past
one of the many
squirreled away between the logs

she will turn it over in her hand
perhaps test it with a small sniff
and think back way back
to what once was
last summer long ago
soothsayer of what will begin again
come spring

—*Julian A. Waller*

Wisti-Twisti

once there was a shop
with a barber pole —
the wisti-twisti as cummings
calls it — and it was
a refuge for the men and boys
in those days before suffrage

and you'd walk in and take
a seat 'midst the sound
of the strop
and the hair falling
and the men would chat
and the boys would listen
and sometimes they'd strike up
harmonies
and all was peaceful
if you can believe a lie

and the women — ah yes
the women — did their
beautifying somewhere else
in a place that always
smelled funny

but these days we all wait together
with magazines whose names
I never heard before
and nobody sings and you never
see a wisti-twisti anymore

which is too bad because
I never got to figure out
where that twirly ribbon
came from at the bottom
or where it went to
on the top

—*Julian A. Waller*

In Chelsea, MA

the guy on the street
with the roses
he runs and he runs
when the light turns red
when the line of cars stops
he runs and he runs
selling roses for $10 a bunch
roses red against a blue sky
roses red in the rain
roses red flecked
white with snow
roses red as he runs
from car to car
$10 a bunch
only $10 a bunch
OK I'll take seven
the kids at home
are hungry but
they can't eat roses
$7 and they can eat
yes $7 and they all can eat
$7 here's your change
and then he runs

—*Julian A. Waller*

Passerine

There were birds abundant,
We were told, on this
Distant northern isle.
But the spare and random trees
Stood bereft and at a loss.

Behind the grinding wind, silence crackled
Like a boot on a frozen puddle. Yet,
I heard the absent voices: chaffinch question,
Sotto voce; pensive mutterings, robin's
Soliloquy in the leafless hedge.

Square Icelandic houses, close, wary,
Stood down the North Atlantic gale,
Whose blade, honed on lava crags,
Scored their stolid grey faces,
Snagged their sanguine tiles.

Reykjavik's red roofs behind me,
I turned to face the bitter sea,
Whose grizzled hide shuddered and
Swelled beneath the charge
Of the berserker wind.

There, on those silver hackles, rode
Velvet white, velvet black,
Eiders, eyes averted,
Pulling against the current to be
Just offshore.

And scoters, a few, silent
Sentries, grey-cloaked,
Marking time in a galaxy
Of snowflakes. With eiders and scoters
I had to be content.

Seabirds expectant of,
I thought, an undertow, while the wind
Sought to drive them beyond the strand,
Strangers to their native land; beyond
Options of season, of tide.

Sixty-six degrees north,
Where the earth drank in milk
Poured by the pagan priest, and ghosts
Of the Althing faltered in endless re-enactments
Of Sagas on the steaming fells.

Ten years have passed, and by
Whatever currents we are
Blown off-course, I find myself
On Vinland's unraveling shore,
Still seeking songbirds.

For flash of tail coverts,
Flit of wing bar, for
That swelling of silken gorget;
Attuned to echoing lyrics, bent
On an imminent aubade.

At my back, wanton continent,
This foreign country
Of my birth. Before me
The self-same sea tugging threads
Of boundaries lost and over-grown.

Leaving the last house on the edge
Of a soporific village, whose
Clapboard cottages, windows boarded,
Opiate through the New England winter,
I wend through press of laurels to the beach.

Where is the flame-
Cheeked warbler, the winter
Wren, whose long song
Garlands the brittle queen
Anne's lace, the frozen rushes?

Silence bleeds
Across the snow, along the shore
Gripped by granite and ice.
The footing is doubtful here,
Among broken rushes,
Cowering stonecrop.

It is New Year's Day.
Against the rise, fall, and rise
Of swells, holding her own,
With rhythmic strokes
And fervid pulse,
One small brown duck.

—Marcy Willow

Song of Spring

Marcy Willow

The lipless mouth sucked in the card. Toneless beeps acknowledged her personal identification number; then 'please wait.'

Her son stretched up and clung to the stone sill. His small fingers were as white as the marble.

"May I do it?" he said.

She lifted him up. "Push this one," she said. There was another beep, 'please wait,' and 'balance of account.'

The numbers were low, but they might change. There had to be more than that.

She lowered her son to the pavement. Machines make mistakes. Wait.

Their closeness held her — her eight-year-old daughter against her arm, her four-year-old son brushing her hip. Market day sounds rose and fell. What if there were a queue forming behind her, waiting for the machine? She kept her eyes on the screen.

The automatic teller machine stood, adamant, between marble pillars that had once framed a window. Words appeared: 'Do you need more time?' She waited in a weft of expectation. The whine and grind of traffic permeated the façade, into her fingertips.

Her daughter touched the back of her hand.

"May I do it?" she said.

She took a long breath, and said, "Yes. Push this. Now this." The mouth ejected the card. The machine dispensed, with a clamor of beeps, a ten-pound note. The children smiled at their mother. They had money. They could buy things. She folded the note and pushed it deep into her skirt pocket.

They held hands and crossed to the market square. They wended through passageways clogged with shoppers.

"Can we get ice cream?" the boy said.

They stood between a barrow hung with hats and one heaped with brown and black handbags. The corners of the note felt sharp through her skirt. She rubbed the top of the boy's hand with her thumb.

"Not now. Maybe later," she said.

He scuffed his shoe on the cobbles. The girl looked away. Her eyes followed the line of chimney pots against the grey May sky. A pigeon flew out of a broken window at the top of the bank building.

She led them through the maze of barrows: turnips and carrots, T-shirts and sandals. They went through a roil of music that for a moment submerged the cacophony of buyers, sellers, and traffic. They bought a loaf of warm brown bread. They stopped to eat a chunk of it on the steps of the war memorial. The World War I soldier stood behind them, his resolute and anxious hands clasped round his rifle. Below him, a weathered, ruddy-cheeked, woolen-clad farmer arranging primroses along a bench, looked up to smile at them.

They went to the post office. The children lingered at the toy shelves. Their mother went to the stand-up desk. She pulled an unfinished letter from her pocket and smoothed the wrinkles.

We are all fine, she wrote.

The words on the page seemed large and awkward. Her hands were cold. She held her fingers against the side of her neck, feeling the steady warmth, the tremulous cold. She looked out the window. Through the window a dusty street sparrow appeared on the pavement. The diminutive busker hopped from side to side and chirped.

They had heard the long Pan-song of a wren on Sunday. The next day they had found the wren, lying in the gravel on the roadside. She shut her eyes, then opened them again to her letter. She wrote:

I thought I heard a skylark this morning ... I did not see it ... .

"Look at this, Mum."

"Just a minute," she said.

She wrote: ... *roses bloom everywhere along our path* ...

"Mummy, look."

She sealed the missive, then held on to it as long as her fingers could go into the post box. She let go.

The boy had a green dragon, the girl three tiny dolls held to a card with an elastic band.

"Those are nice," she said.

Elephants, giraffes, polar bears, and curly-haired dolls thronged the first shelf. Wind-up cars were on the second shelf. The top-most shelf held an old, sagging box cloaked in dust. She stretched and tapped at the box with one finger. It slid over the edge into her hands. She pulled the lid off. Two smaller boxes were inside. Each bore a picture of a red and green parrot. She opened one. A shiny red harmonica tumbled into her hand.

Besides themselves and the clerk, there was only one other person left in the room, a farmer in flat cap and muddy Wellies, writing. She turned toward the wall and put the instrument to her lips. The metal was cool, the wood warm. Her soft breath emerged as a languid hum.

"What's that?"

"May I see it?"

Their shining eyes flitted from hers to the harmonica and back to her — green elfin eyes, round blue eyes. She handed the boxes to them.

"Oh, can we get these?"

"Can we afford these?"

She looked away, to the stoic polished desk, to the tousled rack of greeting cards, to the silver-haired clerk who looked back at her and smiled.

"Mine is gold!"

"Mine is red!"

The children skipped. They skipped ahead. They dodged people on the pavement. They managed to change direction in mid-air. They wound ribbons of music around their mother 'til she thought she must be a maypole.

They could play. She was surprised. They played tunes that had never been played, tunes that swirled and billowed across the square. But they really should play more quietly. Such polyphonics might be noise to other people, to the plodding shoppers ballasted by bulging plastic bags, to the striding businessmen, neckties flapping, looking far ahead. An old lady paused, shifted her bent fingers on the handle of her shopping basket, and said:

"What lovely music."

"Don't play those in here," she told them when they entered the market. They played softly in the tea aisle, loud by the crisps. They played around a man who stood in the middle of the aisle with a hand basket that held one small jar of marmalade. He patted the boy's head.

They took the steep path down to the main road. She stopped to tie knots in the bag handles. She fingered the change in her pocket. The milk and oats would last.

They followed the wall around the cathedral, down to the rows of shrubbery. A chorus of rose bushes, adorned in pink, red, yellow, and white, fanned each other with perfume. They crossed on the zebra-stripes. They turned down the road where the cherry trees stood, pink parasols aloft. The children played cherry blossom music. Pink petals showered onto their heads.

At the river, they stopped in the middle of the bridge and leaned over the rail. A flourish cascaded to the islet below. Dry reed stalks rustled and parted. Yellow-and-brown ducklings tottered out of the rushes. The mother duck, balanced on the crenellations of a crumbling stump, muttered and shuffled her peach-colored feet.

They reached the rising green common.

"Say we're in magic land," the girl said.

The three were carried across the swells of green on melodious gusts. She stopped to switch the heavy bag to her other hand. Such music! All for three-pound-ten.

"I'm a magical princess," the girl said. She leaped through the bracken and brambles.

"And I'm a magical teenager!" the boy said. He turned his cap around backwards.

They led her through a tangled copse. Gangling cow parsnip, taller than she was, leaned toward them like curious youths in white straw boaters. The path narrowed. They stepped over and on shoots of stinging nettles. Her ankle stung from the touch of one fiery claw. They came to a stile. They went over.

A cold wind caught them up in the lane. They stayed close to the stone wall. Lilac reached over the wall, shivering, wet, and fragrant. The children breathed in notes sweetened with lilac. They were saying:

" ... and when we play, the lilac jump off and start to dance down the lane ... "

They twirled like lilac. They quivered like lilac. They breathed out perfumed chords.

" ... and the dandelion fairies dance away on the air ... "

"It's the Song of Spring."

" ... and when we play, the bluebells dance ... "

" ... and the bluebells ring their bells!"

They walked with a dancing walk.

" … and the rocks roll along … "

She put both bags in one hand. She let her fingers brush along the face of the old stone wall; over crisp lichen, into crannies of tremulous fern. A red cow put her head over the wall. Her gaze, in parentheses of horns, followed the children. Their mother's hand glided through the cow's warm sigh.

They crossed the lane, climbed the fence, and dropped onto the pasture. Their arrival brought a clarion call from the geese. The children called back. Young roosters raced up and nipped at the shopping bags. A hen and her chicks waited farther off. The children and their mother broke up a handful of bread and tossed bits as they made their way up the slope to the house. The sky grew heavy and bent beneath a shawl of dark clouds.

They were prince and princess, working on their cardboard castle. They raised their standard over the kitchen table. She spooned steaming oatmeal into bowls.

"Mummy, would you like half my kingdom?" the boy said. His blue gaze met hers.

She set the milk bottle on the table.

"Yes. Thank you. I would."

They sat in their bed, beneath a covering of books and blankets. The girl drew and wrote in her sketchbook. The boy played his harmonica and looked out the window. His eyes followed the swallows diving in the twilight. The wind shook the pane. She opened the window, just a crack. She sat on the foot of the bed and took the pins out of her hair. The boy's music blended with the faraway song of a linnet. Her hair tumbled down onto her back.

The girl sat writing. The boy slept. The red harmonica lay on his lips. She took it and put it under the blanket by his shoulder.

"We have to put the light out now," she said.

The girl slid beneath the blanket with her book. The gold harmonica gleamed between the pages.

CONTRIBUTORS

Judi K. Beach's poems have been published, anthologized, aired and broadcast. She is Coordinator of Regional Contacts for the International Women's Writing Guild. Her poem, *Names for Snow*, was published by Hyperion Press for Children in fall '03.

Diane Berlew started writing seriously after attending a DIWG meeting. She has taught preschool, and worked as a counselor for emotionally disturbed adolescents. She ran a B&B in Stonington, where she has lived for 23 years. She particularly enjoys writing children's stories based on those told to her by her father.

Anne Larkosh Burton moved to Burnt Cove in Stonington three years ago, where she takes instructions in relaxation techniques from her orange tabby, Bobcat. She writes poetry and personal essays and is presently working on a Spiritual Odyssey. In a former life she worked as a Family Therapist and Pastoral Counselor.

Sucha Cardoza came to writing through acting, which she studied in New York with Irene Dailey and New Mexico with the late Kim Stanley. Her teachers, with whom she also worked and taught, continue to inform her life as a writer. She lives on Little Deer Isle with her dogs.

Sandy Cohen, experimental psychologist, explored the neuroscience of human perception. Combining his love of art and music, Sandy helped pioneer the new art form, visualization of music, which he taught at San Francisco State University and UC Berkeley. He writes short fiction and essays. Sandy lives with his wife, Edee, on Little Deer Isle.

Jean Davison is an anthropologist who has spent much time in Africa. She holds a doctorate in International Development/Anthropology from Stanford University. She's the author of several books, including *Voices From Mutira: Change in the Lives of Rural Gikuyu Women*, and *Gender, Lineage, and Ethnicity in Southern Africa*. She splits her year between Harborside, Maine and Austin, Texas.

Maureen Farr I still dream about a road trip to all those little towns that time forgot. Every day, I struggle with my muse. Some days, I win. This fall, my 5-year-old granddaughter and I are taking the Silver Meteor from Penn Station to Florida to explore Longboat Key for a week.

Hendrik D. Gideonse Retired: University Professor, Dean, collective bargainer, twice school trustee, accreditor, research administrator, U. S. Senate aide. Current: Political volunteer, Brooklin (ME) Committee for a pier, Hancock County Community Reparations Board, Selectman. Personal: writer, walker, sailor, builder, gardener, mentor, friend, proud father of two, and Hogan's alpha dog.

Brenda Gilchrist wrote, illustrated, and designed four books published by Braceypoint Press, Deer Isle, including *Paws for Peace* and *Gabi's Doggone Totally Awesome Guide to Maine*. After thirty years in art books publishing in New York, she moved to Deer Isle year round in 1990. Her work has appeared in the *Maine Times*.

Nancy Dobbs Greene Soon after arriving on Deer Isle ten years ago, Nancy Greene found herself writing poems — a surprise since prior to that she wasn't drawn to poetry. She became a regular at the Deer Isle Writer's Group, her training ground, and now also writes personal narrative and short stories. She is a clinical counselor who works with children.

Gayle Ashburn Hadley is an alumna of the University of Michigan. She pursued her writing habit while teaching in or directing programs for inner city low-income children. She now resides and writes on an island off the coast of Maine. Excerpts from *Eternal Vigilance* were read at the 2003 Stonecoast Writers' Conference.

Barbara Hattemer Educated at Smith College and Harvard Business School, Barbara has summered on Deer Isle all her life. She authored articles in *Parents Magazine*, *Yankee Magazine*, *Guideposts*, *World and I*; wrote *New Light on Daycare Research* and co-authored the book, ~~Don't~~ *Touch That Dial: The Impact of the Media on Children and the Family*.

What set **David Hayman** on his road to academia was his hope to become a poet, rather naive at the time. It also got him to Europe, where he continued to write, rather lamely. While there, he opted for a French doctorate. The career move turned him into a critic and buried other aspirations. It was only with his arrival in Deer Isle as a summer resident and his contact with the writers' group that he felt once more the creative tingle. Now, when not working on Joyce and Beckett, he writes the occasional poem or story, truly occasional, only when moved, but with deep pleasure and the inevitable pain.

Crystal Neoma Hitchings Crystal was created by the sensual experiences of environment, from the hot, sweet blueberry fields and summer mud-puddle wallows of her youth to the scraggled spruce forests and water-salted skin of her adult years. Her writing explores this unseverable connection to past and to physical place that describes Downeast Maine.

Nancy B. Hodermarsky, of Deer Isle, itinerant teacher in Rome, Athens, New York City, Cleveland; attorney for safe crackers, broken lives, broken marriages in western Massachusetts; daughter, sister, wife, mother, grandmother and poet, has studied with Stephen Dunn and Robert Farnsworth at Stonecoast and MWPA workshops in Maine, published in *US1 Worksheets*.

Billie Hotaling My life has included several creative activities: teaching, children's mental health work, writing, painting, dance, music, and raising four children. Two published books, *Count the Stars Through the Cracks*, and *Be Like the Bats*, were rewarding endeavors. New York, New Jersey, Vermont, Ohio, and now, happily, Maine have been home.

D Immonen began writing poetry in college, then concentrated on music therapy, education, and performance. She spends the best part of each year on the edge of Burnt Cove and the remainder in Providence, Rhode Island.

Judith Ingram has been a professional visual artist for forty years and also has spent many years writing poetry and short stories. Often, she has incorporated her poetry and sections of her journals into her paintings.

Stuart Kestenbaum has lived on Deer Isle since 1989 and is the author of two books of poems, *Pilgrimage* (Coyote Love Press) and *House of Thanksgiving* (Deerbrook Editions).

Cordis B. Lichten, of the Blue Hill area, explores the dimensions of hope and spiritual quest in adventure fiction with the objective of telling a story that entertains, encourages and reinforces the reader, that resonates long after the last page has turned. "Trough and Crest" is from an unpublished novel.

David Lund, a native New Yorker, has been a devoted summer resident of Deer Isle since 1962. His work as a painter and a poet has shared similar concerns. Over time, the tones of the paintings and poetry have increasingly shared a dialogue. His paintings, known for their evocative imagery and color, are represented in national collections such as the Corcoran Gallery, the Baltimore Museum, and the Whitney Museum.

Deborah Wedgwood Marshall Desendant of the great potter, Josiah Wedgwood, schooled by Quakers, she attended the University of Florence, Italy. A lifelong writer, she has been rejected by *The New Yorker*. She spent all her summers in Sargentville. Returning 34 years ago, she lived in a tree house for 20 years. She now lives on Little Deer Isle with her boyfriend of 22 years.

Jacqueline Michaud's work has appeared in *New Laurel Review*, *New England Review*, *American Letters & Commentary*, *Florida Review*, and *Voices from the Robert Frost Place*, among other anthologies. A frequent guest reader on Maine community radio's WERU-FM, her first collection of poems, *Metropole Café*, was published in 2004 by Mayapple Press.

Elisabeth Reed is a writer who lives in Brooksville, Maine.

Stephen Rifkin A New Yorker and teacher, I lived a long and beloved period of my life on Deer Isle. I attempt to make language and breath so that they may liberate findings. These are poems. Poems assert stirrings of mind, soul, and other imaginings. They are revised to life.

Norma Sheard's poetry has appeared in many journals including *NY Quarterly*, Piedmont, Florida, Maryland & Cape Rock *Review*'s; *Animus*, *Puckerbrush*, and *USI Worksheets*. Born in rural NJ, she received a 1989 NJ State Council on the Arts Poetry Fellowship. She received a 2004 residency at The Millay Colony, Austerlitz, NY.

Julian Waller has been a summer resident of Deer Isle since 1989 and a member of the Deer Isle Writers' Group since 1995. He also lives in El Cerrito, CA and does sculpture and poetry on both coasts, since retiring as Professor Emeritus of Medicine at the University of Vermont.

Marcy Willow is a fiction writer who writes poems every now and then. Winner of Bridport Prizes for Fiction and Poetry, short-listed for the Arc Literary Prize, she has an MA in English Literature, and an MFA in Creative Writing. She teaches writing, recently finished her second collection of short stories, and is working on a novel.